"Darlin' . . . hand? I can't

Harlan's voice, Beth thought. How long since she had conjured up his deep, sexy drawl? Years, probably.

Beth flopped back onto the couch not wishing to face the truth. The truth was she had conjured up his voice, his laughter, his smile – the feel of his body curved around hers as they slept – night after night since she had watched Harlan's Thoroughbred, Stubborn Yankee, win the Kentucky Derby last spring.

"Beth, you're there. I know you are."

This was madness. She wouldn't listen. In the morning, she would telephone a psychiatrist. It was the only thing left to do.

"Beth, I'll break down the damned door if I have to!"

She tore open the attic door. There he was – six feet two inches of taut muscle and Tennessean charm. One of the most eligible men in the south – smart, easygoing, tawny-haired and rich.

"What the hell are you doing here?" Beth demanded, not sure she really wanted to know.

CARLA NEGGERS
is also the author of

CLAIM THE CROWN

and in
Temptation

TRADE SECRETS
FAMILY MATTERS
ALL IN A NAME
A WINNING BATTLE
FINDERS KEEPERS
WITHIN REASON

That Stubborn Yankee

CARLA NEGGERS

MILLS & BOON LIMITED
ETON HOUSE, 18-24 PARADISE ROAD
RICHMOND, SURREY TW9 1SR

*First published in Great Britain in 1991
by Mills & Boon Limited, Eton House, 18-24 Paradise Road,
Richmond, Surrey TW9 1SR*

© Carla Neggers 1991

ISBN 0 263 77559 3

21 – 9111

Made and printed in Great Britain

Prologue

HE WOULD BE SAFE in Vermont.

It was an odd thought. Laughable, even. Harlan probably would have laughed, but for the pain in his head, his eyes, his jaw, his mouth and his abdomen. Especially his abdomen. Bruised, broken and exhausted, he had gotten off the midnight milkrun to Montpelier in the next town over from Millbrook, Vermont. Standing in a noxious cloud of black bus fumes, he had considered his idiocy: had no cash, and no ID. Thugs were out looking for him. A sensible man would have called the police, or at least seen a doctor.

Instead he had pushed up the sleeves of his black polo shirt and trudged the five miles to the outskirts of Millbrook, the picturesque, New England home town of the one-time woman of his dreams.

Elizabeth Stiles.

Mean as a snake, dangerously beautiful, and his first true love. They were married for three short years and hadn't seen each other in nearly ten.

If he had stopped at a phone booth and called, would she have come and picked him up?

Beth had always been a woman to approach with caution. There were things she could have done if her ex-husband had called her at midnight—the least of which was just to hang up on him. Harlan's new-found caution compelled him to avoid downtown Millbrook, where, even in the dead of the night, local gossips might alert his ex-wife to his presence. He had tried hitchhiking, but his bruised face, hobbling gait and the overnight case he clutched to his chest seemed to put drivers off.

He needed to consider the men who had bruised and beaten him and forced him to flee New York. There was an off chance that they'd posted someone in his ex-wife's hometown, in case he showed up. He didn't want to be found. Not yet. Not on their terms. He liked to think his motives weren't merely self-serving; he didn't want the hoods who'd given him the beating of his life anywhere near Beth.

Not that she wouldn't handle herself just fine. If she didn't go after them with an ax, she would hand him over.

"It's my ex-husband you're after?" he imagined her saying. "By all means, take him!"

Still hobbling, he urged himself on with the knowledge that he hadn't much farther to go. Char, Beth's best friend and new sister-in-law, had written him several weeks ago to inform him that Beth had bought Louie Wheeler's old place.

Remember? He's the old geezer who thinks the world went to hell when they invented flush toilets. He's retired to Miami now and has his own hot tub, God forbid. Beth paid too much for the place. She's into being a pioneer Yankee. Beth says we're all too soft. Honest, Harlan, I think she reads the encyclopedia at night and takes cold baths in the morning. She's turning into a curmedgeon.

Harlan grumbled his agreement. Beth Stiles had been a curmudgeon at age twenty. A hellishly sexy one. Irresistible to a southern gentleman like himself. *I know I'm sticking my neck out*, Char had written in conclusion, *but Beth believes there isn't a man alive who can stand to live with her. Mind you, she doesn't think there's a thing wrong with her. It's men who're the problem. Prove her wrong, Harlan. Beth needs you.*

Marriage to Beth's older brother Adam had addled Charity Bradford's brain and turned her into a hopeless romantic, Harlan thought. Elizabeth Stiles had managed fine for nine years without him in her life, and she would be the first to tell him that. She didn't need him. As for *wanting* him—that was the stuff of fantasy. Predawn limps through Vermont notwithstanding, he considered himself a practical man.

He remembered exactly where old Louie's place was located: it was on a back road west of town, where more than two hundred years ago, Yankee pioneers had carved out fields for their cows and vegetables. The maze of stone walls and the giant sugar maples flanking the narrow, dirt road testified to the strength of character and the capacity for hard work of the men and women who had settled that harsh land. Beth viewed their lives as role models for her own and glossed over the history of her own ancestors, who'd been well-off for generations.

Harlan stumbled and collapsed from weakness in the cold, dew-soaked grass alongside the road. His overnight case, the one item that the hired thugs hadn't taken, only because they hadn't seen it, slid down the embankment. He lay there, exhausted and disgusted with himself. He should have had more sense than to slink off in his hour of need to an ex-wife long shed of him. It would serve him right if he died of exposure and stupidity under a rusting, barbed-wire fence.

He heard the rumble of an approaching auto-mobile. Edging down the embankment on his back, he scooted under the barbed wire, close to his over-night case and the stone wall. If the thugs tracked him to Vermont, they'd have no qualms about taking ad-vantage of the isolation of the back road to finish their job on him. Dying of exposure and stupidity was one thing; dying at the hands of those charming individ-uals was quite another. And this time they wouldn't miss his suitcase.

The car was coming fast, kicking up rocks and dust on the narrow road. There was something familiar about the sound of its engine. Something that grated on his nerves. It flew past him, a streak of sea green, rust, bald tires and bodywork not seen on the streets of America since the early days of the Beatles. Harlan gritted his teeth, as Beth's 1965 Chevrolet Bel Air sped down Maple Street toward town.

If he could have been sure she wouldn't run over him, he'd have crawled to his feet and flagged her down. Not the smartest decision he'd ever made—seeking sanctuary with a woman who might want to hurt him more than the men who already had.

Still, he had nowhere else to go. And if he played his cards right, she might never find out he was in close quarters.

1

LEGS ACHING and lungs burning, Beth was relieved to turn the corner onto Maple Street and complete the last stretch of her ten-mile run in the shade. The next house would be hers. Thank heaven. She felt sweat pouring into the bandanna tied around her forehead, and down her back, matting her mango-colored shirt to her skin.

Home. Her house. Her place. No more renting, no more waiting. At thirty-four she had entered the world of home ownership.

"Shack ownership, you mean," her older brothers, Adam and Julian had joked.

That was their opinion. She had hers. The eighteenth-century converted carriage house had a roof, paned windows, wide-board pine floors and charm galore. So what if it lacked central heating and hot water!

The real selling point had been its location. It was situated on a knoll, surrounded by fifty rolling acres of the fields, woods and stone walls of northern Vermont. Beth would have lived in a lean-to to get that picture-postcard view.

If only she didn't have Harlan Rockwood to thank.

That galled her no end. Her ex-husband had been unusually and mysteriously charitable in selling an interest in Stubborn Yankee, his now-famous thoroughbred, to Char. Without Beth's knowledge, Char had invested virtually every cent of her own money and twenty thousand dollars of Beth's savings in the promising three-year-old. Beth had only learned about Char and Harlan's agreement *after* their horse had won the Kentucky Derby. To her mind, it was a deal with the devil. Nevertheless, her share of the winnings—which she'd demanded Harlan fork over at once—had enabled her to buy Louie's old place.

After winning the Kentucky Derby, Stubborn Yankee had gone on to win the Preakness, but had fallen short of the Triple Crown when he came in second in the Belmont Stakes. Beth hadn't taken to having a horse named after her. Right there on national television, Harlan had told reporters that he used to call his wife "Stubborn Yankee." He hadn't said "ex-wife." Adam, Julian and Char all said that was because he had ideas about a reunion with her. She could see it: *"Here she is now, folks, my two-legged, stubborn Yankee."* She'd have to wear her leather chaps and L. L. Bean boots.

She rationalized that Harlan hadn't referred to her as his ex-wife because—Southern aristocrat that he was—he considered public discussions of divorce an unseemly business. Never mind that they had been divorced for nine years. Her brothers and Char remained unconvinced.

Almost three months later, they still wouldn't admit they were wrong. Of course, they were. Harlan Rockwood had backed out of Beth's life as abruptly as he'd bulldozed his way into it. She didn't demand that her brothers and best friend recant, since that would have involved an admission that *she* had *him* on her mind. Too damned much for her taste.

This obsessive thinking about Harlan had to stop! Harlan had gone into that deal with Char and had named his horse after Beth just to aggravate her. Nearly a decade after their divorce, he was finally getting in his digs for all the trouble she had caused him during their three years of marriage. Except in bed. She had never caused him a bit of trouble there. Nor he her.

"Will you stop!" As she came up to her driveway, she kicked a loose stone, sending it skidding wildly.

"Hey," a man's voice drawled, "be careful there, Sugar."

Sugar?

Snapping out of her daze, Beth saw a tan Ford Taurus parked behind her infamous 1965 Chevrolet Bel Air. A sturdy, short man with steel-wool hair was shutting the Ford's driver-side door.

Two of her mutts lapped at his hand; the third was up on the porch, fast asleep. Her half-dozen Rhode Island Reds scratched in what passed for a yard. She didn't see a sign of any of her cats. So much for her oft-stated rationalization for taking in strays: not one was worth a damn at watching the place while she was gone.

The stranger smiled graciously as Beth walked toward him. "Almost got me," he said with a cheerful wink. "My name's Sessoms, ma'am. Jimmy Sessoms."

The sugar, the ma'am, the accent, the name. Beth glanced at the car's license plate and wasn't surprised to see it was from Tennessee.

She tugged the bandanna off her head. Ten miles had taken their toll on her hair, as well as the rest of her. She pulled the covered rubber band off her ponytail and let her sweat-dampened locks fall loose onto her shoulders.

"What can I do for you?" she asked warily.

She saw Sessoms run one hand slowly across his lower jaw and look from her to her house. The previous owner, Louie, a seventy-five-year-old widower, had given up on the yard some thirty years ago. The barn out back had been crumbling for the better part of the century. The outhouse, which had satisfied Louie, but at which Beth drew the line, was in fine shape.

Sessoms narrowed his eyes, trying to reconcile what he saw—the house, the animals, the Indian paintbrushes dotting the knee-high field grass of her yard—with what he had presumably expected to see. Beth didn't care to explain that she had moved in to Louie's old place only three weeks ago and hadn't yet gotten around to the outside. Or that exercise and her body had had an uneasy relationship for years, and she was entitled to sweat. The man would come to his own conclusions.

"You're Mrs. Harlan Rockwood?" he asked.

Now it was Beth's turn to narrow her eyes. Even when she had been married, no one had ever called her Mrs. Harlan Rockwood. It wasn't her style. For his part, Harlan hadn't given a damn what Beth called herself. But Eleanor Rockwood, Mrs. Taylor Rockwood, had had her own ideas. Her mother-in-law had given her stationery with Mrs. Harlan Rockwood embossed at the top in elegant lettering. Although Eleanor had never openly challenged Beth, she'd always introduced her as Mrs. Harlan Rockwood and made it plain that she considered Beth's decision to be called by her own name as another sign that she would never be a Rockwood. It hadn't seemed to occur to her that Beth didn't *want* to be a Rockwood. She was just in love with one. In retrospect, the tension over the Rockwood name had been a symbol of her three-year struggle to retain her own identity within her marriage.

On that score, she had succeeded only too well.

Beth saw Jimmy Sessoms eyeing her closely. She wiped the perspiration off her face with her bandanna and tried to look more like an Olympic athlete and less like a thirty-four-year-old woman bound and determined to stay in reasonable shape. She was fitter than she had been in years. Nevertheless, ten-mile runs were ten-mile runs, and no breeze-through!

"My name's Elizabeth Stiles." Her clipped words stood in marked contrast to his drawl. "Harlan Rockwood and I are divorced."

Sessoms nodded. "I understand. Mind if we go inside?"

Beth hesitated. She wanted to know why this competent-looking man with his thick, middle-Tennessee accent had driven up to see her. She could make a guess: Harlan must have sent him. But why? Who was he? Not a Rockwood lawyer, for sure; they all wore bow ties. Someone involved with the Rockwood stables? Last fall one of Harlan's trainers had tried to swindle him by switching one of his most promising thoroughbreds—in which he'd sold a share to Char—for a dead ringer. The switch had sent Char into near bankruptcy. To make amends, Harlan had let Char invest in his favorite horse, Stubborn Yankee.

In fact, Beth had only found out about that deal when the time came for her to collect her share of Char's profits. However, since the Kentucky Derby, she had begun to suspect Harlan had another scheme in the works.

Was Jimmy Sessoms involved?

She felt her muscles stiffening and was already regretting missing her cool-down stretch. "Mr. Sessoms . . ."

"I'm a private investigator," he said quickly. "From Nashville. Your mother-in-law, Mrs. Taylor Rockwood, hired me. Please, Mrs. Rockwood, it's very important that we talk."

Beth balled up her bandanna in one hand. "What about Mr. Rockwood? Taylor, I mean."

"He's not associated with this."

Jimmy Sessoms withdrew his wallet, showed her his ID, and quietly repeated his request that they go inside and talk. Unembarrassed by the ramshackle condition of her house, Beth led the way. She had only been able to accomplish so much in the three weeks since she had moved in. The entire first floor was maybe as big as the Rockwood foyer, if she included the attached woodshed. There was an eat-in kitchen of 1930s vintage, a pantry and what Louie had called his "great room," which served as a living room and bedroom. Beth's first order of business had been to have a bathroom installed. Next was getting hot water. After that she planned to convert the upstairs into a proper bedroom with a dormer, to take advantage of the view. Right now she could still see hay marks on the old, rough-hewn walls. Some noisy rodent was up there, waking her at night. It sounded bigger than a mouse. In her brothers' opinion, she should tear the place down and put up one of Mill Brook Post and

Beam's high-quality houses. As a vice president, she could get a sizable discount. Her brothers shared her keen interest in old houses, but hers, even she had to admit, didn't qualify as an antique.

Beth pulled a pitcher of iced tea from the refrigerator, a refugee from the fifties.

"You live here?" Sessoms asked.

"Yep."

"Summer place?"

Beth shook her head and got down two tall glasses from the open shelves above the sink, added ice and poured the tea, while Jimmy Sessoms took a seat at her round table, covered with a blue-and-white-checked cloth. She had deliberately placed the table in front of the window, with its spectacular view of the valley and mountains beyond. Despite the uneven floor and peeling wallpaper, the place was homey, she knew, if not Rockwood elegant.

She sat down in a white-painted, wooden chair across from the private investigator. "So what's this all about?"

"Mrs. Rockwood—"

"Ms Stiles," she said emphatically. "Please call me Ms Stiles."

"When was the last time you saw your husband?"

"I haven't seem my former husband in years. Why?"

"You owned an interest in Stubborn Yankee, didn't you?"

"A very minor interest, arranged by a friend without my knowledge. I never actually talked to Harlan or even saw him. What's this all about?"

Sessoms drank a mouthful of tea. She watched him resist making a face: it was peppermint tea. "But you communicated with him?"

"Not in person."

He sighed. "When's the last time you saw him in person?"

Jimmy Sessom was being cagey. Beth doubted she'd get anything substantive out of him until she gave him a satisfactory answer.

"In person? Let me think."

Not that she had to. The last time she'd seen Harlan Rockwood was nine years ago this September, on the seventh. The date was embedded in her memory, because it was the day her marriage had officially come to an end.

It had also been the last time she and Harlan had made love—for old times' sake, they had told each other. That steamy afternoon was far more deeply embedded in her memory than any other. They had made love so passionately, so exquisitely that Beth wasn't likely ever to forget her last day with Harlan Rockwood. Even with their marriage over, she found herself wanting him as much as ever. And the feeling had been entirely mutual. She could still see Harlan, walking stiffly toward his car after their twelve-hour marathon.

"I haven't seen Harlan since our divorce," she told Sessoms.

"Nine years?"

"That's right."

"You're sure?"

"Mr. Sessoms, I assure you I'd remember if I'd seen Harlan."

No question of that. No doubt they'd have ended up in bed together. It had been that way between them right from the beginning. A long time ago Beth had decided that if she was going to get on with her life, she would have to stay away from Harlan Rockwood. She supposed that if they had spent more time on working out their problems and less time in avoiding them, they might have understood each other better. Hindsight was always twenty-twenty, and understanding didn't necessarily lead to reconciliation.

"I've answered your questions," Beth said, losing patience. "Now what's this all about?"

Jimmy Sessoms frowned. "Mrs. Rockwood . . . Ms Stiles." He sighed again, shaking his head. "I'm afraid your husband's missing."

Beth let the "your husband" slide and sat forward in her chair, feeling strangely afraid. "What do you mean?"

"Five days ago—last Sunday—he was to meet his mother for brunch. He never showed up. Since then she's made every effort to locate him, without success."

"Did she call the police?"

"They're not worried. Neither is anyone but Mrs. Rockwood. Apparently Harlan travels a great deal and isn't always easy to locate. Certainly the idea of a thirty-seven-year-old man forgetting a brunch date with his mother isn't unheard of. Mrs. Rockwood disagrees."

Beth tried to make herself look nonchalant. "What do you think?"

The investigator shrugged. "A woman, probably."

Naturally. Aware of an unexpected sinking feeling in her stomach, Beth nodded. She blamed the feeling on drinking iced tea too soon after her run. Harlan hadn't remarried. For years she had told herself she'd sleep easier when she knew Harlan Rockwood had married another woman.

"That makes sense," she said dispassionately. "So why come to me?"

Jimmy Sessoms looked amused. "I figured you for that woman."

"Me?" She laughed. "Mr. Sessoms, Harlan and I married young. We've been divorced for a long time. I don't think kindly of him, and he doesn't think kindly of me. If you suspect he's gone off with a woman, you'd better forget me and concentrate on someone southern, on someone who knows her china and silver patterns."

"I don't know . . ."

"Well, I do. Have you met Harlan?"

"Not yet."

"If you'd had, you could have saved yourself a trip north."

"Maybe." He pushed away his iced tea as he rose. "Maybe not. But if you'll excuse me, ma'am, what I've learned about Harlan Rockwood so far makes me think he rather likes a woman who sweats."

Beth could feel her shirt sticking to her back.

"If you hear from him, give me a call." Sessoms placed his card upon the table. "My answering service knows where to reach me. Okay?"

"Of course, but I won't hear from him. Not after nine years."

He shrugged. "Crazier things have happened. Good day, Mrs. Rockwood." He grinned at her cheekily and corrected himself. "Ms Stiles."

AFTER JIMMY SESSOMS had left, Beth showered and put on an oversize T-shirt and a pair of shorts. She dug around in her refrigerator for her last beer. There had to be one in there somewhere. A six-pack lasted her forever. Apparently not this time. Instead she fixed herself a gin and tonic and went onto the porch.

A summer's late afternoon in southern Vermont couldn't be beaten. She sat on the old porch rocker and propped her bare feet upon the railing. The sagging porch would need to be replaced. There wasn't any hurry. Appearances were other people's concern, not hers. She had the view, the sounds of the birds, the feel of the wind on her face. What more could she possibly want?

All the same she felt strangely uncomfortable and dissatisfied.

What had happened to Harlan?

Was Jimmy Sessoms right? Had Harlan disappeared on her account?

No way. If he had, she would have known about it by now. Notwithstanding Char and her brothers' opinions on the matter, Harlan hadn't decided to rekindle a relationship with her after nine years. The fact that he hadn't remarried simply proved he liked his independence as much as she liked hers.

Second question. Had Harlan disappeared on account of some other woman?

"Nah," she muttered, taking a sip of her drink.

Harlan wasn't one to act irrationally because of some woman. Disappearing on purpose was not his style. It was also inconsiderate, and Harlan, for all his faults, wasn't inconsiderate. If another woman was involved, Jimmy Sessoms wouldn't have driven a thousand miles to Vermont to track down the ex-wife of the man he had been hired to find.

In all likelihood Harlan had forgotten his brunch date with his mother and gone off on one of his trips without mentioning it to her. He was a big boy. He didn't have to tell his mother every little thing. But even if he had forgotten, surely he would have remembered by now and called to apologize.

That left the fourth possibility.

Harlan hadn't disappeared by choice.

Beth shivered, suddenly feeling very alone. Silly. No one was going to come after *her*.

Jimmy Sessoms had.

How selfish, she told herself, to worry about her own safety when Harlan . . .

When Harlan what?

Harlan Rockwood was a wealthy man. As the owner of the thoroughbred that had nearly won the Triple Crown, he had recently received a great deal of national exposure.

Had someone kidnapped him?

Beth raced inside and dialed the number on Jimmy Sessom's business card. Getting his answering machine, she left a message she immediately regretted. She had sounded so panicked and breathless. Sessoms would naturally assume that she cared about what happened to Harlan Rockwood.

She pounced on the phone when it rang.

"Your hubby called?" Jimmy Sessoms inquired.

"No, of course not. I told you, his disappearance has nothing to do with me. Mr. Sessoms . . ."

"Jimmy," he corrected her.

"Is there any evidence of foul play?"

He chuckled. "Foul play?"

Beth didn't share his amusement. "You know."

"Yes, ma'am, I do, and if there was, do you think Mrs. Rockwood would stand for the police *not* getting involved?"

Not a chance. "What's your next step?" Beth asked.

"Ms Stiles, if you want to hire me, you'll have to wait your turn."

"I'm curious. Harlan and I may not be on speaking terms, but that doesn't mean I don't care if he's been kidnapped."

"Who said anything about kidnapping?" Sessoms asked sharply.

"I didn't mean to imply..."

"If you know something, let's have it."

Beth was silenced. Suddenly she wished she'd poured herself another drink instead of having left that stupid message for Sessoms. "I don't know anything," she said coolly.

"Well, this thing doesn't even begin to play like a kidnapping."

"Then what does it play like?"

There was a short pause. Then Jimmy Sessoms, his humor apparently returned, drawled, "Plays like a man trying to get his wife back."

"Ex-wife."

"If you say so."

"I have the papers...." Beth stopped herself. The man was incorrigible. "Why doesn't this thing play like a mother overreacting?"

"You have met Mrs. Rockwood, haven't you?"

Enough said. Eleanor Rockwood wasn't the hysterical type. "What does she think?"

"All I can say, Ms Stiles, is that I drove up here to Vermont at her suggestion. Now if you want to know more, you call her."

"Wait, I—"

But he had already hung up.

Beth knew Taylor and Eleanor Rockwood's telephone number by heart. It was one of those things that stuck. To be sure, she and her former mother-in-law hadn't spoken since she and Harlan had announced their plans to divorce. Eleanor hadn't taken the news well. She had always considered her son's marriage hasty and ill-conceived, making no secret of her belief that Beth was too young to give up her life in Vermont and settle down in Tennessee. Even four years as an undergraduate at Vanderbilt University in Nashville weren't enough to prepare her for a life so far from home. That had been Eleanor's opinion when she was being charitable. On a more gut level, Beth knew that Eleanor had disliked her daughter-in-law's directness and her clipped, no-nonsense manner of talking. Most of all, she'd disliked Beth's determination to have a career and her disinclination to follow in her mother-in-law's footsteps.

None of this, however, was ever stated. Beth had just known it.

She'd also known that Eleanor was a traditional woman who preferred to avoid failure and even a whiff of scandal. She'd probably loathed having to tell her friends that her son and his Yankee wife were divorcing. Divorce was all right for other people, but not for the Rockwoods.

"Why?" she had asked her son in Beth's presence. "What happened?"

"We just think it's for the best," Harlan had replied, refusing to air the dirty linen of their marriage in front of his mother.

Eleanor had then turned to Beth. "And what do you think?"

Beth had repeated Harlan's words. Later she'd discovered that Eleanor blamed Harlan for not having had better control over his emotions and marrying Beth in the first place.

Now all that was ancient history, and regardless of what Eleanor Rockwood had believed, she had had nothing to do with Beth and Harlan falling in or out of love with each other.

Beth picked up the phone and dialed the Tennessee number.

Eleanor Rockwood answered.

Beth all at once felt like an idiot and hung up. Then she felt like a bigger idiot and dialed again.

"Mrs. Rockwood? Hi, it's Elizabeth Stiles. That was me a minute ago. My cat knocked over the phone."

"Beth," Eleanor Rockwood said, sounding as formidable as ever. "How nice to hear from you."

Chitchat wasn't Beth's style so she got right to the point. "Jimmy Sessoms was here."

Beth heard her ex-mother-in-law inhale. Eleanor Rockwood was very, very good at repressing her emotions. She said tensely, "Then you know about Harlan."

Deciding to play Eleanor's game, Beth struggled to control her own confused feelings. "Yes. Jimmy Sessoms told me. I wish I could say Harlan was here with me. I mean, I don't . . . you haven't heard from him?"

"No, I haven't."

"May I ask you one question?"

"Of course," the older woman replied, everything apparently under perfect control again.

"Did you have any specific reason for thinking Harlan might be with me?"

"Beth, you must understand that I would prefer not to discuss family matters."

"Please. Nothing Harlan's done has ever been simple. I don't mean to sound cavalier. I'm trying to get a handle on this situation, in case I can help."

Eleanor sighed. "Thank you, Elizabeth." Her tone was polite and distant. "If I require your assistance, I'll be sure to ask. I do appreciate your concern."

"Okay. If I hear from Harlan, I'll let you know."

"How very kind."

Feeling nosy and stupid for having called, especially after Mrs. Rockwood's coolly civil goodbye, Beth fumed for ten minutes. Finally, she put on a skirt, a cotton blouse and a pair of sandals, and headed into town for supper. To console herself, she indulged in a high-calorie meal, ordering a big bowl of New England clam chowder with hot corn fritters and, for dessert, wild blueberry pie.

Where was Harlan?

You don't care, she told herself, and promptly tried Jimmy Sessoms again when she got home. He didn't return her call.

She then dialed Taylor and Eleanor Rockwood's number again. This time Taylor answered. Beth had gotten along reasonably well with Harlan's father. Taylor had been too preoccupied with running the family businesses to concern himself with what kind of car his daughter-in-law drove, or whether his son was happy. Taylor Rockwood had apparently realized straight off that they'd never make a Rockwood of her, and had never been inclined to beat his head against a brick wall.

They exchanged pleasantries. Her former father-in-law was clearly surprised to hear from Beth. Trying to be more tactful than usual, she explained that she had heard from Jimmy Sessoms and was worried about Harlan. Instinct told her not to mention her earlier conversation with Eleanor. She'd only end up sounding defensive.

"Who's Jimmy Sessoms? What's happened to Harlan? Beth, I don't mean to be rude, but I have no idea what you're talking about."

"Isn't Harlan missing?"

"Missing what?"

"Missing. You know, disappeared."

"Not that I know of, no." Taylor hesitated, and Beth wouldn't have been startled to hear that he was wondering whether she'd gone crazy in the past nine years. "Where did you get such a notion?"

"Then where is he?"

"With you, I thought. Isn't he?"

Beth frowned. "Mr. Rockwood, I haven't seen Harlan since our divorce."

"Hmm. Well, maybe he changed his mind." Sounding as though he was talking to himself more than to Beth, he murmured, "I'm sure there's no cause for alarm. Is Jimmy Sessoms a friend of his?"

"No..." Beth decided against squealing on Eleanor. Let her tell her husband herself that she'd hired a private investigator.

"I don't wish to cut you short, Beth, but Eleanor and I are on our way out."

"Mr. Rockwood, what made you think Harlan was with me?"

"Don't you think you should take that up with him?"

"I would if I could find him," Beth said, more snappishly than she would have liked. She always felt so out of control among the Rockwoods. But what was that snake in the grass Harlan up to?

"So you don't know where he is?" Taylor inquired.

"No."

"But he told me . . ." Beth heard Taylor clear his throat once again. It sounded as if *he* wasn't going to overreact. "I understood he would be contacting you. He missed a brunch date with his mother on Sunday, and we haven't heard from him since. I just assumed he was acting on his promise."

Now they were getting somewhere. "What promise?"

"It's not my place to say, but—well, obviously something's wrong here. On Saturday evening at a dinner party, Harlan told me he had one Stubborn Yankee in his stables. Now he just needed one back . . ." Taylor paused, then finished, "back in his house."

Beth bristled. She'd lay money that Harlan hadn't said "house."

"He'd had a few glasses of wine, you understand. He doesn't normally . . . er . . ."

"Compare me to a horse?" Beth inquired acidly.

"Well, no. But you should be complimented. Stubborn Yankee is a beauty."

"I'll remember that, next time I look in the mirror. Did he say anything else?"

"Not really, no. Beth, you don't think anything's happened to him?"

"I don't know what to think." That much she did know. "You sure he was coming my way?"

"I was," Taylor Rockwood said, not sounding sure any longer. "Perhaps I should talk to my wife. Does she have your number?"

"I doubt it," Beth said politely, and gave it to him.

After she hung up, she flopped back onto her couch. A cat crawled onto her stomach and she said, "Harlan, you son of a bitch. Where the hell are you?"

From the dark recesses of her house his voice drawled, "Right here, darlin'."

2

BETH WENT ROCK-STILL and listened, then sat up straight on her couch and looked intently around the room.

A light over the sink in the kitchen and the floor lamp next to the couch in the great room illuminated the downstairs of the small house, but left the corners in shadows when dusk fell.

The couch bisected the large room, separating her living quarters from her sleeping area. She climbed onto her knees and looked over the back of the couch into the shadows of what had become her bedroom. A double-sized iron bed was piled high with old quilts. Standing next to the bed was Louie's massive, marble-topped dresser with an attached mirror. Having an iron bed in the middle of the living room had rather a dampening effect on her entertaining, to be sure. Housecleaning, however, was a breeze.

The arrangement also made it tougher for apparitions to hide.

The cast-iron potbelly stove occupied the middle of the far wall, near the bathroom Beth had installed. If she was truly paranoid, she would have to inspect the bathroom and the attic before she was satisfied she hadn't been hearing things.

Harlan's voice. How long since she had conjured up his deep, sexy drawl? Years, probably.

Not true.

She sank back and pulled a quilt over her feet, not wishing to face the truth.

The truth was that she had conjured up his voice, his laughter, his smile—the feel of his body curved around hers as they slept—night after night since Stubborn Yankee had crossed the finish line and won the Kentucky Derby that spring.

"Darlin' can you give me a hand? I can't get the door."

This was madness. She wouldn't listen.

"Beth, you're there. I know you are."

In the morning she would telephone a psychiatrist. It was the only thing left to do.

"Beth, I'll break down the damned door if I have to!"

Something was kicking at her attic door; the wrought-iron latch and hinges vibrated. Beth jumped up, jarred out of her stupor.

"Harlan Rockwood, I swear I'll . . ."

She tore open the door, half expecting thin air. There he was, seventy-four inches of taut muscle and Tennesseean charm. One of the most eligible men in the South—according to an article Char had clipped and sent Beth during her own brief stay in Rockwood country. Smart, easygoing, tawny-haired and rich were the words used to describe Harlan. What more could a woman want?

His lanky frame became visible as he stiffly walked down the narrow, steep attic stairs. He was wearing jeans, a rumpled pale yellow cotton shirt that appeared to be buttoned up crooked and socks without shoes.

"What the hell are you doing here?" Beth demanded, not sure she really wanted to know.

"Catching my breath. Want to give me a hand?"

"No, dammit, I don't want to give you a hand! I want you out of there—"

"Beth, I can't."

"What do you mean? Move it, Rockwood. I don't like the idea of having strange men holed up in my attic. Now march."

He sighed. "I'll need a hand."

"What, afraid my stairs'll give out?"

She grabbed his forearm and helped him down the stairs, even as she wondered about this helpless act. One thing Harlan Rockwood wasn't was helpless.

"Didn't think all my working out was going to come in handy jerking my ex-husband around," she grumbled, heaving him against the doorjamb. "Honestly, Harlan. People are looking all over for you, and here you are—Harlan?"

He couldn't speak. She could see that. He had sagged against the doorjamb, wincing, as pale as death.

"Oh, Harlan," Beth breathed. "What now?"

No longer fuming, she could see how his jaw and left eye were split and swollen. Coagulated blood and purple and yellow bruises marred his handsome, aristocratic face. He hadn't shaved in several days, and his tawny hair stuck out in the wrong places.

He was clearly in a great deal of pain. He held one arm across his abdomen and tried to smile. "It's nothing serious."

"Are you going to be sick?"

"No."

"The bathroom's right behind you if you are."

"I know," he said.

She knew she sounded snappish and decidedly unsympathetic. Well, why not? If anyone had told her that morning that by nightfall she'd have fended off a private investigator, called her in-laws and hauled her ex-husband down her attic stairs, she'd have either taken the first plane out of Vermont or laughed herself into a padded cell.

She recalled having nursed Harlan back to health after more than one good pummeling.

As social as ever, he added, "I'll be fine."

"Then go in and have a seat. I'd like to know what's going on around here. My God, Harlan. If you didn't already have a fat lip, I'd probably give you one. How long have you been upstairs?"

"A couple of days."

"A couple of days!"

She gritted her teeth. No, she wouldn't let Harlan get to her. If she had to put another thousand miles between him and herself, she would. She would sell Louie's old place and move to Quebec. She'd . . .

"I'm going crazy," she muttered, watching Harlan limp to the couch. No, she wasn't going to let him get to her. He was on her turf now, something he had managed to avoid throughout their marriage. Harlan had repeatedly joked that the Civil War statue on Millbrook Common was the meanest-looking Yankee he had ever seen and a serious deterrent to his peace of mind in her hometown.

Harlan eased himself onto the couch and patted the spaniel's head. The tabby cat jumped up at once and curled up on his lap. Harlan scratched her ear.

The squatter had obviously made a few friends in the past two days.

"I want you out of my house," Beth told him.

He glanced up at her. "I'd like to explain."

"Nope. I'm not getting sucked into whatever mess you're in. No way. You have your things upstairs, I assume? Allow me."

Ignoring his pain-wracked cough, Beth climbed the stairs to the attic. A naked bulb threw seventy-five watts of light into the center of the large, unheated room. Two eyebrow windows brought in little light, even in the daytime.

Harlan had apparently managed to transform ten square feet under the light bulb into serviceable living quarters. Beth's old sleeping bag was spread out on a twin-sized mattress she had stored. A footlocker served as a table. One of Louie's cast-off metal lawn-chairs sat in the best light, with Beth's copy of *Scaramouche* hanging open over the arm. Harlan had set one of her pottery plates on the floor, and an empty Chinese food container stood next to it. There was the empty bottle of her last beer! Presumably he'd remembered that whatever went into their refrigerator never came out again in recognizable form.

His leather suitcase lay open at the end of his makeshift bed, everything in it neatly packed. Beth closed it and hauled it downstairs.

She plunked it at his feet.

He sighed. "You have no idea what it cost me to get that thing upstairs."

"Missed your valet, did you?"

"Beth, you know I don't have a valet."

While she'd been upstairs, he had gotten ice for his face, wrapped it in a plastic bag and applied it to his swollen eye.

Beth didn't give him any sympathy. "If you've been here a couple of days, you must be on the mend. I can have your bag sent, if you can't carry it."

"How charitable," he said dryly.

"It's the best you're going to get from me."

"You'd throw an injured man out into the cold, cruel night?"

"It's not cold, and about the cruelest thing out there is a sleeping chicken. Besides, you, Harlan Rockwood, aren't just any injured man. You're my ex-husband—a sneak." She clenched her fists at her sides, the shock of seeing him wearing off and the full measure of his effrontery sinking in. "I want you out of my house."

He kept the ice on his blackened eye. "You're over-reacting."

"That's what a man says when he knows he doesn't have a leg to stand on." She jerked her thumb toward the front door. "Out."

He didn't move, and Beth was reminded that Harlan Rockwood had never done anything in his life he didn't want to do. When it suited him, he could be remarkably single-minded. "It hurts to walk," he said.

Beth was unmoved. "I'll help you."

"I'd collapse before I made it out of your driveway."

"Then I'll scrape you up in the morning."

He half smiled. "You talk a tough game, Beth darlin'."

"Don't you 'Beth darlin'' me. Harlan, I'm not kidding. Look at it this way, you have a better chance of staying alive out in the 'cold, cruel night' than you do staying in here with me."

"Classic hyperbole," he said dismissively. "The last two days, your various critters around here and I have been talking, and we agree that for all your talk about skewers and stewpots and whatnot, at heart you're a big softie."

Being called hard-hearted would have offended her less than being called a big softie. Harlan knew that. She crossed her arms over her chest and assumed a grim expression—the one she used when her dogs and cats assumed they had equal access to her counters.

Harlan didn't exactly run for the door. Calmly and deliberately, he removed the ice from his eye and gazed at his ex-wife. He didn't say a word. He had wonderful eyes, even when they were rimmed with black and blue bruises. Nine years had added sprays of lines at their corners, but had not lessened their spark and vitality. They were emerald green, darker around the irises. Eyes that had once seemed capable of penetrating to her very soul.

"Give me until morning," he said softly, all wryness gone. "Then I'll be out of your way."

Beth didn't want to give him another five minutes, never mind until morning. It wasn't a question of being hard-hearted. It was a question of self-preservation, of maintaining the precarious and treasured balance she had established in her life. Already it was teetering. She had been thinking far too much about Harlan Rockwood these past weeks. By morning he could be back under her skin. Then what?

"You don't have a good effect on my life, you know," she admitted.

"Sorry."

He wasn't sorry. He loved it, she knew. Back in Nashville all those years ago, he had relished stirring up her life. She was the nose-to-the-grindstone Yankee; he was the easy-going southerner. Of course, it wasn't that simple. Nothing ever was. Intelligent, athletic and scion of a family that had ventured down the Cumberland River deep into Tennessee with the Robertsons and Donelsons, Harlan Rockwood often fooled people with his deceptively easygoing manner. It had taken a while for even Beth to realize he was every inch a Rockwood.

Looking at his swollen, blackened eye and his bruised and bloodied jaw, she knew she couldn't kick him out into the night.

"All right." She could hear the surrender in her voice. "You can stay the night. I want you out of here by 7:00 a.m. Don't talk to me. Go on back upstairs, and I'll pretend you're not here."

"I thought you wanted an explanation," he said mildly.

"Changed my mind." She spun around, headed for the kitchen and dug around on top of the refrigerator for a bottle of aspirin. She returned with it and a glass of water to the great room and handed them to Harlan. "There. Don't think I'm hard-hearted."

"I don't have to think it, I know it." But he took the water and aspirin. "Going upstairs hurts even more than coming down."

"Should have thought of that before you snuck into my house."

"I didn't sneak in. The door was unlocked."

"Because there isn't a lock. I can assure you there will be one by noon tomorrow."

"You're peeved because I pulled one over on you. I've had the run of your place for two days and you didn't even know it." Some of the old fire blazed in his eyes. "That galls you, doesn't it?"

"Not really." Harlan Rockwood couldn't put her over the edge, not anymore. "I've been putting in long hours at the mill. *I* know that hard work can make a person too tired to notice somebody creeping around in their attic."

"Call that an attic, do you? Feels more like a hay-loft. It's a comfortable little place you've got here." He stretched out his long legs, obviously disinclined to move. "Except for your tub. I tried the shower, but nearly froze before I realized there was no hot water. So I followed your lead and tried that galvanized washtub of yours. I don't fit in it as well as you do."

"You spied on me?" Beth asked hollowly.

"Didn't mean to. There's this little hole above the kitchen, next to the old chimney. I heard this racket—kettles whistling, dogs barking, scuffing and slamming—and thought I'd better investigate. There you were, easing yourself into a washtub of suds."

Beth just managed to keep herself from going after him with her poker. "Upstairs or out of here. Now, Harlan. I don't want to know anything. I . . ." She inhaled deeply, trying to control herself. "Up or out."

"As you wish."

He slowly climbed to his feet, appearing, if possible, even more worn and battered than before. A boxer in college and law school, he had endured his share of beatings. That had been a long time ago. Now Harlan Rockwood was closing in on forty and the owner of world-renowned thoroughbred stables. After all, what did she know about him anymore?

He was a stranger.

She reddened at the thought of having this man— this stranger—peering down at her in her washtub in the middle of her sagging kitchen floor. Thank heaven for all those weeks of conditioning! She was trim and solid, and even if Harlan had seen her naked, it couldn't have been that sorry a sight.

Small comfort that was.

"You can make it upstairs without my help," she declared. "If you've been prowling through my cupboards for two days, you've managed before."

"Only because I knew you'd have just rolled me outside and let me rot like a dead cat if I'd collapsed."

"No. I bury dead cats."

To her annoyance, he grinned at her. "Your bark's still bigger than your bite, Beth darlin'."

"Don't count on it. You collapse and see what I do."

He hobbled to the attic door. Beth didn't move as she listened to him mount the steep, narrow stairs.

Then she heard a curse and the unmistakable sound of a lanky Tennesseean tumbling down seven steps. Harlan groaned and cursed as he fell. Beth raced over to the base of the stairs.

He was stretched out across several steps, still hanging on to the railing, which had become dislodged from the ancient wallboard. His gray color and the variety of curses coming from his oh, so proper mouth indicated he wasn't faking. Picking her way through chunks of plaster and railing, she climbed the steps and crouched next to his chest.

"Are you all right?" she asked.

He managed to glare at her, a good sign. "No, dammit, I'm not all right!"

"I withdraw the question." He was clutching his chest. "Ribs?"

He nodded painfully. "Think I cracked a couple."

"Right now?"

"No—before."

Before. *Someone* had given Harlan Rockwood a good thrashing. Beth was thankful that he wasn't planning to tell her who. She shuddered at the prospect of being drawn into Harlan's troubles. Accidents didn't happen to Harlan Rockwood, and he was never a victim. "Lucky you didn't puncture a lung," she said.

"Trust you to put a pleasant spin on things." He groaned as he tried to adjust his position, then gave up. "Give me a second to catch my breath...."

"You should have told me you had cracked ribs. I'd have driven you to an inn instead of making you go back upstairs."

"Such a saint."

"Come on." She looked for a spot to grab hold of to help him to his feet. There wasn't a man alive whose body she'd known better than this one's. "Let me give you a hand."

His pain-wracked gaze fastened on her without amusement. "Going to kick me the rest of the way downstairs?"

"I might, if you don't quit talking about me like I'm some kind of sadist."

He came close to a smile, even if it was a nasty one. "Florence Nightingale you aren't, m'darlin'."

He slung one long arm over her shoulder and pulled himself into a sitting position. He let go of the loosened railing. Harlan had always been remarkably stoic about physical injury. Staying crouched, they managed to get downstairs without further incident. Beth ignored his curses and tried to ignore the feel of his sinewy, male body against hers, focusing on the task at hand. *I cannot get sucked back into this man's world. I have got to send him packing.*

At the bottom of the stairs, Harlan removed his arm from Beth's shoulder and made his way to the couch on his own. To her dismay, she had to admit that nine years had not diminished his raw sexuality. She'd just have to disregard it.

His face pallid, he slumped back against the cushions and shut his eyes. "Why didn't you just kill me?"

She shrugged. "I figured quick and painful was better than slow and painful. Shall I call a doctor?"

His eyes opened and fixed on her with seriousness. "No."

A chill went through Beth, and she looked again at her ex-husband's battered face. "You're in some kind of trouble, aren't you?"

He sighed.

"Never mind." Beth began to pace, folding her arms across her chest in a futile effort to ward off her anxiety. "I don't want to know. I'll do what I can to get you on your feet and out of here."

"I'm sorry." He winced. "I shouldn't have come here."

Unable to stop herself, she asked softly, "Why did you?"

He half smiled. "I'd had the hell beaten out of me. Where else would I go?"

The hospital, the police and a hundred other places. He was attempting to charm her.

Beth felt herself weakening.

"If I can get my chest wrapped and rest a bit," Harlan said, "I should be all right."

With brisk efficiency, Beth helped him off with his shirt, which could have used a spin through a washing machine. She tried not to dwell on the dried blood on the collar and sleeve.

"Sure you didn't just get run over by a train?"

Harlan didn't answer. His breath was warm on her face as he slipped off his shirt, blanching in pain. He wore no undershirt. His chest and shoulder muscles were more developed than Beth remembered. She attempted to regard him impersonally, but couldn't. Objectivity for her where Harlan Rockwood was concerned was impossible—and a primary reason why she had never gotten in touch with him after their divorce. With no children, they had easily gone their separate ways. *Had* to stay separate and whole and get on with their lives.

If she had tried to stay in touch, maintaining the illusion of an amiable parting, they'd have kept on landing in bed together. How could she ever have fashioned a new life for herself tied, however tenuously, to her former husband?

"I'll see what I can find to wrap you with." She jumped to her feet, glad to put herself at a safer distance from him.

Given her zest for physical fitness, she had a drawer full of various sizes of Ace bandages. She grabbed three and returned to Harlan, half wishing he had been an apparition and had vanished. There he was, stretched on her couch, battered, beaten and impossibly sexy. A good thing he had cracked ribs. Without them, they might have ended up together in her iron bed.

Unexpectedly, Harlan was all business. "Tell me about your visit from Jimmy Sessoms," he said as Beth briskly began wrapping his chest.

"You didn't eavesdrop?"

"Tried, but I didn't want to risk moving, in case either of you heard me upstairs. If you'd taken him in here instead of the kitchen, I'd have heard more."

"I'll remember that next time," she said sarcastically.

Since there was no reason not to, Beth repeated her conversations with Jimmy Sessoms and with Eleanor and Taylor Rockwood.

When she finished wrapping and talking, she sat back on the floor. Harlan looked thoroughly absorbed by his thoughts. Beth yawned. It was getting late, and she had to be at the mill early in the morning. How much did she want to know about the trouble Harlan was in?

How much did she *need* to know?

"I'd forgotten that comment I made to my father," Harlan said after a few minutes. "I should never have involved you, Beth. I had no idea Mother would hire a private investigator. I thought Vermont was the last place anyone would look for me. If I could leave now,

I would. But I wouldn't get far, and I can't risk having anyone find out I came here, for your sake."

Beth felt increasingly jittery. "Then you want me to pretend I never saw you tonight?"

His expression was graver than anything she had ever seen on the face of fun-loving Harlan Rockwood. "Yes." Then he leaned toward her, reached down and took her hand in his. The effort drained even more color from his face. "7:00 a.m. Then I'll be out of your life for good. I promise."

The *last* thing she needed was Harlan Rockwood back messing around in her life, and yet his words made her feel unreasonably sad and alone. Disregarding her ambivalence, she said, "Okay, it's a deal."

"I'll just stretch out right here," he went on, "and sleep on the couch, if you don't mind."

"You're too tall. You can sleep in my bed." Then she added quickly, "I'll sleep on the couch."

He squeezed her hand and managed to smile. "Sleeping in your bed without you would only frustrate me."

She smiled. "Even now?"

His sad, sensual smile seemed to express his own sense of loss. "You mean after nine years or in my condition?"

"Both."

"Nine years is a long time. I don't mind telling you I've never met a woman like you, Beth. Whatever went wrong between us, we did have our moments.

As for my condition . . ." He winced when he tried to move, then grinned that luscious, rakish grin of her dreams. "Hell, I'd die happy."

She covered him with a quilt. "Enjoy the couch."

HARLAN AWOKE AT DAWN feeling stiff and sore and more miserable than he had in years. Sleeping on the couch mere yards from Beth had brought its own measure of frustration. He threw the old quilt she'd covered him with onto the floor. He had to have been insane to come here. He couldn't have anticipated Jimmy Sessoms's visit; nonetheless, he should never have taken the risk of involving his unwilling ex-wife in his problems. It was inexcusable—an act of desperation and selfishness.

He had to get out of Vermont.

He was bruised and broken, all right. The pain in his chest had lasted through the night. At least his facial wounds were showing signs of improvement. He could probably manage to eat a decent breakfast today. Those two mornings listening to Beth hum and putter around in her kitchen had been more than he could bear. She would listen to a news program on public radio while she made coffee and pulled together breakfast.

Listening to her bathe at night had been sheer torment.

Of course, he hadn't seen as much of her in the washtub as he had pretended last night. Not nearly enough. The angle was all wrong, and as much as he hated to admit it, he was too much of a gentleman to spy on an unsuspecting lady. Besides, if Beth had caught him, he'd have ended up in far worse shape than he was now. He grabbed his shirt and slipped it back on, leaving it unbuttoned.

Across the room, her brass bed was a tumble of ratty quilts, one dog and two cats. Obstinate and opinionated though Beth might be, no one had ever made him feel quite so alive. No one had ever matched her fiery spirit—or her ability to annoy him.

Harlan knew he should be on his way, but he had to have one last look. She was lying on her side, her tousled, sandy hair covering most of her face. She had on an electric-blue T-shirt nightgown, twisted and pulled tight across her breasts. He could see the outline of her nipples against the soft fabric and felt himself stirring, remembering.

His gaze lingered on the curve of her shoulders and arms, and he saw how fit and strong she was. He had always admired her boundless energy. In her habitually half-buttoned work shirts and jeans she appeared very, very sexy. None of *that* had changed. What you saw was what you got. Some people didn't understand her honesty, considering her unmannerly and unbecomingly direct, preferring pretense to a laugh that was sometimes too loud and opinions that were sometimes too strong and uncompromising.

Beth had never been good at minding her manners. In fact, she had never even bothered to try.

Ancient history. Even nine years ago, Harlan hadn't concerned himself with what anyone else thought about her. It was what she thought about herself and about him that mattered.

He didn't dare touch her. Leaving her while she was asleep was difficult enough. If he woke her, he couldn't be sure he would keep his promise to be gone by seven. It was just after five now.

She was a tough woman, this stubborn Yankee he had once loved. Once? His throat tightened.

He had never stopped loving her. Until her friend Char Bradford had come to Tennessee and asked his advice on horses, he had worked hard at keeping Beth out of his mind. He had gone on with his own life after their divorce, fully expecting to marry again, raise a family and have the kind of relationship that had eluded him with Beth. For better or worse, she had been his first true love. He'd continually compared other women who wandered into and out of his life with his memories of her. He wasn't so much still *in* love with Beth as not *out* of love with her.

Char's arrival in Nashville had changed all that. He'd wondered if Beth had put her friend up to contacting him—if Char's interest in thoroughbreds was a part of a scheme they had cooked up for Beth to subtly worm her way back into his life.

He had been so far off base that he could have strangled himself. Char's interest in thoroughbreds had been genuine. Beth had no more use for her ex-husband than she did for an old pair of shoes. Even less, given her frugal Yankee ways.

In her own way, the thirty-something woman asleep under her piles of quilts and pets was the same beautiful, outrageous and impossible person who'd taken so much pleasure in driving him crazy at twenty. The Beth he had fantasized about wasn't the *real* Beth.

The real Beth hadn't mellowed with age.

One of her tabby cats playfully nipped at his hand. Harlan backed off. No matter how much she could sometimes irritate him, he was acutely aware that he desperately wanted to crawl under that mountain of quilts and make love to Beth, the real one.

It was impossible to believe they hadn't made love in nine long, long years.

He sighed, glad of the distraction of his cuts and bruises, even grateful for the hell of a mess he was in. He hadn't divorced Beth because he had stopped loving her. He had known that then, and he knew it now. He had divorced her because he couldn't bear to destroy her.

He still couldn't.

He left quietly. Outside, he hardly noticed the cool rain. Her 1965 Chevrolet Bel Air started reliably, as it had back when Beth had roared into Nashville sitting behind its wheel.

"No one," she informed him then, "touches my car."

She had let him drive it only once. He doubted her attachment to the old jalopy had lessened over the years, but what was he supposed to do, call a cab?

Apparently the Bel Air was Beth's only mode of transportation. All the same, even if he wrecked her favorite car, she could afford to buy a new one. Her pioneer ways were a deliberate choice. She would be taken aback, to say the least, when she discovered he'd borrowed—she'd say stolen—her car.

By then he'd be long gone.

3

BETH CALMED HERSELF to a slow boil by the time Char picked her up at eight o'clock. In all her years with Harlan Rockwood, she had never been so angry with him as when she'd awakened to the roar of her car engine. She'd gotten to the window in time to see the Chevy backing down her driveway. Harlan had never gotten used to its three-speed transmission. To no avail, she'd run after him. Fuming, she'd briefly considered calling the police, but she didn't want to become a subject of town gossip. Instead she'd called Char.

"Thanks for coming," Beth said as she climbed into her friend's new car. Their winning horse had enabled Char to trade in her old jalopy for a four-wheel-drive Jeep, which she needed with a house in the hills of Vermont and three children. Beth shut the door hard. "It's been a rough morning."

"Where's the Chevy?" Char asked.

"I don't want to talk about it."

"What, it died on you? Don't expect me or anyone else to mourn, Beth. No car can run forever."

"It didn't die on me."

"Then what?"

"Never mind. You didn't tell Adam you were picking me up, did you?"

"He'd already left for the mill." Char flashed her dark eyes at her best friend. "What's the big deal if he knows or not?"

"No big deal. He hates my car."

"Who doesn't?"

To get to the mill, they had to drive through Millbrook Center and Old Millbrook, then past the defunct boys' academy owned by the Stiles family, and now in the process of being converted into commercial and residential space. Beth kept her eyes on the scenery, hoping to discourage Char's questions.

"Isn't that your car?" Char asked.

Beth swung around as the Cherokee flew past Bert's Garage, and Char slowed down. Beth's Chevy was parked near a gas pump. Harlan Rockwood was standing, slightly hunched over, in visible pain, having a chat with potbellied Bert, *the* biggest gossip in town.

Char said, "Well, well, well," and pulled in behind the Chevy.

"Not a word."

Beth leaped out of the Cherokee, and heard Harlan curse when he spotted her. Bert hollered a good-morning as she ran around the front of the Cherokee, squeezing between its gleaming bumper and that of the Chevy.

"Put it on her tab," Harlan said, pointing to Beth as he vaulted into her Bel Air.

"Wait!"

He blew her a kiss as he screeched away from the gas pump.

"Don't I know that fellow?" Bert asked.

"Not now, Bert. I've got to go after him."

"What about the bill?"

She groaned. It was exorbitant. The last few days, she'd been running the Chevy on fumes. If Harlan had run out of gas, it served him right. She thrust a twenty at Bert, then jumped back into the Cherokee.

She looked at Char. "I suppose you're not interested in following him."

"You suppose correctly."

"Told you it's been a rough morning." Beth sighed. "He'd run the Chevy into the ground before he'd give up."

Easing out of Bert's, Char kept her eyes on the road, apparently wanting to avoid looking at Beth. "I don't suppose you want to tell me what Harlan Rockwood is doing in town, never mind driving your car."

Beth let her silence serve as an answer.

WITHOUT A WORD to her brothers about Harlan Rockwood plunging back into her life and stealing her car, Beth struggled to lose herself in her duties at Mill Brook Post and Beam. She wouldn't allow herself to think about Harlan, her car, his bruised face, or the trouble he was in. She failed miserably and spent the better part of the morning brooding.

Ten minutes into her eleven o'clock meeting with Julian and Adam, she sensed they were on to her.

"Beth?" Adam asked.

Beth wriggled in her chair. Caught wool-gathering. That had to be a first. "What?" she asked curtly.

"Do you have anything to add?"

She didn't have the slightest idea what they had been discussing. "No."

Beth and her two older brothers prided themselves on being able to work together on an equal basis. To be sure, Adam was more single-mindedly devoted to Mill Brook Post and Beam than either of his two younger siblings, but that could change. During the past year Beth had seen both her brothers marry. *Anything* could change.

Except me. I've got my house and the mill, and that's it for me. I'm not changing. Someone's got to stay steady around here.

Wishful thinking. The changes in her brothers' lives had transformed her own life. Her best friend was no longer available at a moment's notice to watch horror movies and eat popcorn on a lonely Friday night. Neither were her brothers. They accepted her, but sometimes she couldn't help feeling like a fifth wheel.

Now, on top of everything else, Harlan Rockwood had swiped her car. The one constant element in her life for the past sixteen years was in his hands.

He wouldn't treat her Chevy gently.

No one in Millbrook would be sorry to see her old car go. Half the town said it was an environmental hazard; the other half said it was an eyesore. She could afford a car with a catalytic converter, antilock brakes, automatic seat belts. . . . But she wanted her Chevy back.

Crossing her arms over her chest, Beth flopped back into her chair. It was too quiet. She noticed Adam's hazel eyes pinned on her. She unfolded her arms and sat up straight, smiling and muttering something about the weather. Equals or not, every now and then Adam couldn't resist playing the big brother.

This time it was Julian who piped up first. "What's eating you, Beth?"

"Nothing."

Her answer was too curt. Her brothers gave her their we're-on-to-you look.

"I know things are hectic around here," Julian said. "If you've got a problem, speak up. You're not the type to sulk, Beth. Makes me nervous."

"I'm not sulking." She swallowed, then added more steadily, "I just didn't sleep well. It's this heat."

"Are you getting spooked out there alone in that shack?" Julian asked.

She scowled at him. "No. There was . . . there was a bat in the attic. He kept flapping around and waking me up, so I finally had to get rid of him."

"You shoot him?"

"I wish." She did, too. "No, I threw a blanket on him and tossed him out the window."

Adam gave her a big-brother glance before he spoke up. "What makes you think the bat was a he?"

"Only a male bat would flap around in my attic and keep me awake."

"Not much on men this morning."

Beth started to protest, but stopped herself. A quick mental replay of her morning conversations turned up several unflattering generalizations about men— all, she would argue in her current mood, deserved.

Julian grinned at Adam. "She must have a new boyfriend if she's so down on men."

If Beth had been in a cheerier frame of mind, she would have protested that she got along fine with men, so long as she and they stuck to saws and logs and nuts and bolts and greasy old engines. When she was just one of the boys, she did fine. It was when romance and lust entered into her relationships with men that everything went out of whack. Since she was already in a lousy mood, she didn't rise to Julian's bait.

Adam leaned back, looking every inch the stolid mountain man. Sometimes Beth couldn't believe her best friend had married him. He said, "Why don't you tell us why Char drove you to work this morning?"

"She told you?"

"Yes."

The fink! There had been a time in the past when she could have counted on Char not to give Adam the time of day, much less tell him who'd driven whom to work that morning. Now that Char and Adam were married, Beth had to clue her best friend in on what niblets of their conversation were to be kept private and what weren't. Char was usually closemouthed about most things, but Beth had set herself up by refusing to explain what Harlan Rockwood had been doing at Bert's Garage in her Chevrolet. So Char had sicced Adam on her.

Pretty soon the whole damned town would be wanting to know what had happened to Beth's '65 Chevy. Was it really gone? Beth could hear the applause now.

Either she had to accept the loss of her car or deal with the thief herself. Easier said than done. First she would need more information and a clear head. She had hoped that concentrating on work would get her back on track. Instead, all morning she'd brooded and asked herself unanswerable questions. Who'd beaten up Harlan? Why? How'd he get to her place in his condition? Would she ever see him or her car again? Did she care?

She hadn't wanted to tell Adam or Julian anything about last night. If they didn't laugh themselves silly or, worse, side with Harlan, they'd go after him. She wanted to reserve the pleasure of revenge for herself. She also wanted her car back, and Adam and Julian weren't likely to see that as a reasonable goal.

"I had car troubles," she lied. She had to throw them some kind of bone, because stonewalling and elaborate tales would only confirm that something really nasty was up in her life. Char had apparently kept quiet about Harlan, or Adam wouldn't have waited until eleven to speak up. Beth forced herself to smile. "Let's reschedule this meeting, okay? I need another cup of coffee to clear my head."

A whole pot wouldn't do the trick.

"Okay by me," Julian said. His teasing grin had faded, and she saw her brother study her with concern.

She smiled tightly and started across the wide, pineboard floor of the eighteenth-century mill to her desk.

Behind her, Adam asked mildly, "Your bad mood and that nonsense about a bat in the attic and car troubles wouldn't have anything to do with a Nashville P.I. named Jimmy Sessoms, would it?"

Beth stopped dead in her tracks and her heart raced. All that sidestepping of the truth, and Adam already knew. He had guessed that her preoccupation had to do with Harlan Rockwood.

"I don't know any Jimmy Sessoms."

Since Adam was playing games with her, she figured he deserved the lie.

"He said he'd been out to see you. He stopped by here, after you'd told him you hadn't seen Harlan since your divorce." Adam didn't gloat. "You always were hell as a liar. It seems like Harlan's in a bind. If you're worried about him, I can understand. It's nothing to be ashamed of."

"I'm not worried about Harlan." Her jaw was tight, and she ground out her words in such a way that even she didn't believe herself. "You know as well as I do he comes out of everything smelling like a rose. All right, so this Nashville P.I. did stop by yesterday. I'd forgotten all about it. I informed him he was barking up the wrong tree. I haven't seen Harlan in nine years and don't expect to. If I'm a little distracted this morning, it's because of my car."

"Got it down at Bert's?" Adam asked suspiciously.

"No, not yet."

"What's wrong with it?" Julian inquired, walking up beside Adam. "Must be pretty bad if you can't fix it yourself."

"Look, you two, if I want your help, I'll ask. Adam, what did Sessoms tell you?"

"Same thing he said to you, I imagine. Harlan missed a brunch date with his mother. There was a report he'd taken a beating, and he hasn't been seen since Saturday. Sessoms thought he'd start looking here, because of your stake in Stubborn Yankee. Beth? You okay?"

"Sure. As I said, Harlan will come out of whatever he's gotten himself into just fine. It's certainly no concern of mine."

Beth wondered why Sessoms hadn't mentioned the beating to her. Good-ol'-boy camaraderie? Spare the little lady the sordid details? Possible, but unlikely. Suddenly she wasn't so sure she trusted Jimmy Sessoms. Maybe she should find Harlan before anyone else did.

But to what end? Why did she care?

She cared about her car. Maybe Harlan could manage on his own without her help. She doubted he'd look after a battered, twenty-five-year-old automobile.

HARLAN PULLED OVER at a windy rest stop off I-81 near Scranton, Pennsylvania. The Chevrolet was running like a top, but he needed coffee, ice, sleep and painkillers. His condition was a vast improvement over early Tuesday morning, when he had practically crawled to Beth's house. If he'd collapsed and died en route, it was comforting to know she would have kicked a clod of dirt over him and gone about her business. He wouldn't want to put her out by having her grieve over him.

The woman was the hardest-hearted Yankee he had ever known. That he had turned to her in his hour of deepest need had only seemed to irritate her. Well, he couldn't exactly blame her.

He stumbled from her old bomb of a car and made his way to the men's room, where he splashed cold water onto his face and considered his reflection. Gray-skinned and unshaven, his face looked like that of a derelict. Certainly not that of one of the mid-south's most eligible men. No wonder Beth had sent him packing, though knowing Beth as he did, he supposed that even if he'd been at his handsomest and most charming, she'd never have let him stay the night.

He should have kept away from her in the first place. His thrashing had obviously knocked a few screws loose in his brain. First, he should have known Beth would toss him out on his ear. Secondly, he had no business involving her in his problems.

He bought himself two chocolate bars and a cola before trudging back to the car. He sat on the trunk, hoping that the warm sun and breeze would ease his pain and frustration.

"Oh, Beth," he said aloud.

The candy bars and soda consumed, he slid off the car.

It has to be done. No choice.

He tossed his trash into a nearby receptacle, headed back to the rest area building and located a pay phone. The *gentlemen* who'd pounded his face in had also relieved him of his personal items—except for the overnight case which they hadn't seen—but he had his long-distance credit card number memorized. He dialed the number for Mill Brook Post and Beam.

A receptionist answered and transferred him to Adam Stiles.

"You got out of town with your hide intact, I take it," Adam said dryly.

"Barely."

"I haven't seen Beth in such a lousy mood since you two were married."

There was no amusement in Adam's tone. Harlan said nothing for the moment, wishing the pain would go away. All of it. The bruises, the mistakes, the ache he felt whenever he thought about Beth. Against his better judgment, he'd stopped by Mill Brook Post and Beam that morning. It was a case of either going there, robbing a gas station or slinking back to Beth's in defeat—he needed cash. Adam had given him what he had and asked no questions, seeming to know instinctively that Harlan would sort out whatever mess he was in before returning to Millbrook.

Harlan only wished he'd asked Adam for a car, as well. The vision of Beth diving for her Chevrolet was one that would haunt him for a long, long time.

"What does she know?" Adam asked.

He willed himself to be coherent and concise. Exhaustion, pain and worry were all taking their toll. "Nothing."

"Harlan, maybe you should tell me what's going on. You're in trouble, I know. I saw your face."

"It's a long story." He wasn't going into it now. He'd called Adam for one reason. Several hundred miles of solitary driving had helped clear his head. He knew what he had to do. "A P.I. from Nashville was looking for me at Beth's place yesterday."

"Jimmy Sessoms. He was looking for you here, too. Something wrong with him?"

"Not that I know of. However, if he thought to look for me in Millbrook, so could . . . others."

"Like the meats who beat you up?" Adam's voice was deadly serious.

Harlan briefly shut his eyes. "Yes."

After a long silence, Adam said, "I see."

"Beth doesn't know anything, Adam. Not where I am, what this is all about. Nothing. These people might not believe that. They play hardball. If they find her . . ."

"They won't."

Harlan sank against the phone booth in relief. "Thanks."

"What about you?"

"I'll be fine. I have a better idea of what I'm dealing with now. I won't be fooled twice."

"Doesn't seem to me you can afford to be. I'm here if you need me."

"Thanks."

Hanging up, Harlan felt his sugar and caffeine intake start to kick in. Beth wouldn't approve of what he had done, but he'd had to do it. No fool, Adam would know better than to tell his sister that her ex-husband had asked him to watch out for her. No one looked after Beth Stiles but Beth Stiles herself. She'd made that very clear years ago. Adam would be discreet, and Beth safe. That was the bottom line. Right now, that was all that counted.

Mission accomplished.

Now on to the next one.

HOPING AGAINST HOPE Beth waited for a phone call asking her to come pick up her abandoned car. None came. That meant Harlan hadn't just borrowed her Chevy for a bit. He'd definitely stolen it. Nor was there a phone call from Harlan himself apologizing and telling her what was going on and that he was all right.

Jimmy Sessoms, Eleanor and Taylor Rockwood apparently didn't think to call her, either.

Well, they could all just stew in their own juices. *She* was going on with her life.

She hitched a ride with one of the sawyers and left work early.

Once home, she took off for a long, exhausting run. A quick dinner and the company of her cats and dogs improved her mood. Really, she was doing the right thing. Going after Harlan and her car had seemed rational this morning, but the quiet of the hot afternoon had restored her common sense.

She fed the chickens and hummed to herself as she felt the freshness of a north wind on her cheeks. A Canadian high was moving in, pushing out the heat and humidity. Maybe she'd even stop fantasizing about steamy southern nights and smooth-talking, southern gentlemen. She climbed onto a huge, gran-

ite boulder at one side of the chicken coop and let the
wind swirl around her.

She spotted Julian's truck halfway around the bend
and stopped humming. Her brothers had been acting
decidedly weird and secretive all afternoon. What if
they knew something they weren't telling *her?*

What?

"Why speculate," she muttered, "when you can
ask?"

With a couple of dogs in tow, she marched down to
the end of her driveway, onto the dirt road and around
the bend. She shushed the dogs as they came upon
Julian's truck. They paid her no attention. They were
developing a bad habit of barking when she didn't
want them to bark.

Julian already had poked his head out the window
by the time ... e got there. "Nice evening."

"Why're you spying on me?"

"I'm not spying. I'm just figuring what kind of post-
and-beam house I'd build where your shack is."

She hooted in disbelief. "Don't lie to me, Julian.
You've heard from Harlan, haven't you?"

"No."

"Adam has, then."

Julian stared at her and yawned. Beth peered into
the truck and noted the baseball bat propped up
against the seat. An icy trickle started down her back,
but she suppressed her uneasiness.

"Got a game tonight?" She nodded casually at the bat. Julian enjoyed an occasional turn at home plate with a coed softball team his enterprising wife had put together. When he shook his head, Beth leaned into the window. "Julian, I'm not going home until I get a straight answer. Why are you spying on me?"

"It's not a question of spying."

"If you're not spying, then what?" She stopped and glanced again at the bat, recalling Harlan's cuts and bruises. "I'll be damned. You're *protecting* me, aren't you? You think whoever beat up Harlan might come for me. Damn that man! And you and Adam, too. You have no right to sneak around my house like the secret service and not tell me what's going on." She took a deep breath to calm herself. "When did he call? Or is he holed up at your place tonight? I should have known you men would stick together."

Julian gazed at her calmly. "Talk to Adam if you want answers. He asked me to take a shift keeping an eye on you. He said you'd opened up another can of worms with Harlan and could end up with some heavies coming after you."

"How charming of him to warn me, too." Her sarcasm was apparently lost on Julian, who simply shrugged. She pointed down Maple Street, toward the mountains. "On your way, Julian. I can take care of myself."

"No way. If I left and something happened to you . . ."

"You'd never forgive yourself. Too bad."

He grinned. "No, I'd hate to have to face Adam. He's taking the night shift at ten. Talk to him then."

They weren't going to budge. Obviously they believed her personal safety was threatened. She probably wouldn't stand a chance with whoever had beaten up Harlan. Unfortunately, neither would Julian or Adam.

"There's no point in you two suffering any more than you have to on my account." She straightened. "Hang on a few seconds, while I throw some stuff together. I can camp out at your place tonight, and we can all sleep better."

She called Adam from Julian's house in the woods. Only because she needed information did she remain civil. "You heard from Harlan?"

"Beth, he shouldn't have involved you in whatever mess he's in. He knows that now. All you need to do is lay low for a while, until this thing cools off."

"Where is he?"

"He didn't say. He was calling from a pay phone."

"He still has my car?"

Beth heard Adam hiss with impatience. "Nobody cares about your damned car."

"I do."

"Beth . . . Look, I didn't want to have to sneak around your back or withhold information, but you're not rational where Harlan's concerned. God knows, you have reason not to be. Julian and I are just trying to help."

"Help whom?"

"You, of course."

"Looks to me like you're helping Harlan."

Adam mumbled something that didn't sound at all pleasant. "He called again tonight, if you must know. He says your car's running like a top, and he'll have it back to you as soon as he can. He wouldn't tell me where he is. He's not in Vermont, okay? Let this one lie for a while, Beth. Get some sleep and relax."

"Don't tell me what to do." She slammed down the phone.

Julian and Holly had the good sense to back off and leave her to her own devices after Julian had pointed out the six-pack of beer cooling in the refrigerator. Beth grabbed one and shook open the sleeping bag her sister-in-law had left on the living-room couch. She felt bad about snapping at her brothers. They were helping her out, however ineptly. Had anyone ever known what to do or say where she and Harlan were concerned?

"Harlan, where are you?"

The answer, or perhaps the suggestion of a possibility, came to her in a decade-old dream. She dreamed of Coffee County—a place she had come to love as much as the river and woods of Vermont where she had grown up. When she awoke from the dream, she was strangely agitated, longing to be back in her dream. Throwing off the sleeping bag, Beth padded into the kitchen and splashed herself with cool water. She pulled on a sweater, jeans and sneakers.

She found the key to Julian's Land-Rover hanging next to the side entrance. She scrawled a note and attached it to the door.

> I'm off after Harlan. I need to know what's going on. Don't worry. If anybody was after me, I'd know by now. Tell Adam I'll be in touch. Thanks for your concern. I'll be okay.
>
> Love, Beth.

The sound of the Rover starting up was enough to wake the dead. Julian opened his bedroom window and yelled something unintelligible at her. She shut the driver's side window and let him yell. Maybe Holly would talk him out of chasing after her.

Then again, maybe she wouldn't.

Beth dropped into third, braced herself for a rough ride and peeled out.

Halfway between Julian's house and the mill, she pulled off the road and skidded behind an abandoned red barn. Seconds later, Julian's truck blew past her like the proverbial bat out of hell.

"Sometimes I hate being the little sister."

Beth loosened her grip on the steering wheel and took the long way round to the interstate.

4

"SHE TOOK OFF," Adam Stiles said, his fury—fury at Beth and now at Harlan—clearly audible over the phone lines.

Harlan squinted against the haze of a Tennessee morning and digested what Adam had told him. He could understand the other man's frustration. Time after time Harlan had vowed that he wouldn't let Beth get to him. And time after time she had. The woman was thoroughly unreasonable.

"What do you mean, she took off? Took off where?"

"After you, I should think."

Harlan suddenly became aware of a jump in his heartbeat at the prospect of Beth chasing after him. The response was logical in its way. His heartbeat would quicken if a tiger were after him, too.

"She's crazy," he snapped. "She hasn't the vaguest idea where I am. Anyway, you can't be right. She was ready to give me the boot yesterday morning, I left before she got the chance."

There was a moment's silence on the Vermont end of the line. "You shouldn't have stolen her car."

"I needed transportation."

"I'd have loaned you a car, Harlan, no questions asked, anything to keep you from sending my sister off the deep end. She claims she has no feelings left for you. Yet from her recent behavior, it doesn't appear to be so."

"She hates my guts."

"Is that what you really believe? Char told me about you two at Bert's yesterday morning. Beth regards your stealing her car as a deliberate affront."

"She's wrong." Harlan's jaw tightened. Was Beth out of her mind? How could she have seen it as anything but a desperate act? "I had to get away. Adam— you're sure she left of her own accord?"

"What's that supposed to mean?"

Harlan could hear the sharpness in Adam's voice. "No one . . . grabbed her, I hope?"

"No." Adam's tone was deadly cool. There wasn't a single Stiles whom Harlan would care to cross. "Julian heard her leaving and attempted to catch up with her. Taking off was her idea. Harlan, talk to me. Tell me what's going on."

"You must find her."

"Harlan—"

He hung up abruptly hoping Adam wasn't going to end up siccing the entire state of Vermont onto him. He rubbed his stiff neck and breathed in the smell of freshly cut grass. He was on his own turf. It wasn't much of an edge, but right now, it was all he had.

"I JUST WANTED to let you know I'm fine," Beth told Adam from a pay phone in northern Virginia. It was hot. The Rover's worn shocks had made for a bouncy ride, and doubts had begun to creep into her consciousness about the wisdom of her impulsive decision. Why go after an ex-husband she was well rid of and a car that had seen its best days two decades ago? She had no rational answer.

"Don't worry about me. Just consider this a long-overdue vacation."

"Beth," Adam said tightly, "you're out of your mind. Let Harlan solve his own problems."

"Who says I want to solve his problems? I want my car back."

She heard Adam sigh. "Who do you think you're kidding? If anyone but Harlan Rockwood had stolen that car of yours, you'd be collecting your insurance."

His words cut close to the bone. "It's not insured against theft. Don't meddle, brother, and don't bother thanking me for having the courtesy to call."

She slammed down the phone before Adam could explode. She was tired, cranky and not sure why she'd bothered to call him in the first place. Courtesy? Not likely. The truth was that she'd had to find out if he'd heard from Harlan.

Her back ached from the marathon session behind the wheel. Julian's Land-Rover was no treat to drive. It smelled of grease and sawdust. He wasn't nearly as scrupulous about keeping his vehicles in smooth running order as she was. His primary concern was that they started. Details like shock absorbers and brake pads meant nothing to him.

Resisting the candy and soda machines, Beth did a few stretching exercises before heading back to the Rover. She hadn't eaten in hours, but hunger gave her an edge, she thought, that helped keep her alert. Harlan had enough of a head start on her as it was.

Feeling the heat, she climbed in. She took a swig from her water jug and cranked up the Rover.

Adam was right. She was nuts.

"NOTHING YET?"

The long, long drive south had exhausted Harlan more than he would ever have guessed. The fatigue penetrated his very bones. He hurt. God, he hurt. Now he was deep in the Cumberland Mountains, in the cool, still air of dusk. Almost there. Close to quiet, safety and a soft bed.

He stopped at a country store he'd been coming to all his life and used the pay phone to call Vermont once more.

"No." Adam sounded grumpy. "She called around noon and told me not to worry."

"Any idea where she is?"

"On your trail, buddy. Anything more specific than that, no."

Harlan closed his eyes, feeling dizzy and miserable. "If it's any consolation, she won't find me. No one will."

"Harlan . . ."

"You know I'm not going to tell you any more than that. I made a mistake in coming to Vermont, Adam. I recognize that. Now I'll do what I have to do to keep that mistake from hurting any of you."

"You're just as stubborn as Beth is."

"That isn't a compliment, is it?"

"No. But if you need help, you know where I am."

A STATE TROOPER rousted Beth on her way after she'd dozed for a couple of hours at a rest stop in southern Virginia. It was a warm, fragrant night, reminiscent of so many she'd spent in the south. Giving in to hunger and exhaustion, she bought a coffee and two candy bars at an all-night truck stop and cranked up the Rover as fast as she dared. A dinnertime phone call to Julian had netted her nothing beyond growls about getting her butt and his Rover back to Vermont, pronto. Adam's anger, too, had reached a point beyond words. From here on out, Beth would communicate with her brothers through an intermediary—but not Char. Her best friend had turned into a hopeless romantic since her marriage to Adam.

"If you two don't get each other killed," she'd said, referring to Beth and Harlan, "or kill each other, you're going to realize you're two peas in a pod."

Char was dead wrong, and Beth had told her so. "I'd rather chew sawdust than have anything to do with Harlan Rockwood."

"Then why are you chasing all over the country-side after him?"

"I want my car back."

Char had the nerve to laugh. "By the way, where are you? I know you've been stonewalling your brothers, but you can talk to me."

"So you can rat on me and they can send out a posse? No way."

"Thanks a lot, Beth. I thought we were friends."

"We are, but I'm also your husband's sister. Trust me, Char. Even if you tried to keep my whereabouts a secret, Adam'd guess you were holding back on him, and there'd be hell to pay. I'm not going to put you or me in that position. This is my problem. I'll handle it."

"Well," Char had said, sounding both exasperated and amused, "have fun."

Fun! But a certain peace of mind had descended upon her as she traveled south. She felt surprisingly at ease and in control. At least she had gained a degree of confidence in her mission.

She knew where Harlan was.

There was no question in her mind that she would catch up with him, get her car back and prove to him—and especially to herself—that he couldn't twist her around his finger any longer.

She was free of Harlan Rockwood, and she was going to prove it.

COFFEE COUNTY, Tennessee. In a rolling valley at the end of the Appalachian chain, it boasted some of the most scenic and untouched country in the south. It wasn't a watering hole for the glitzy crowd, but Harlan had never worried about being fashionable. He'd always come to Coffee County to fish and relax, and more recently to be alone. There were memories here of good times, of stupid mistakes, of a woman he had loved and lost.

He arrived at his rustic two-room cabin at noon and immediately collapsed onto the brass bed, not waking until suppertime. He welcomed the quiet. At last he could think. He had Danny at the country store deliver him a mountain of provisions. Danny minded his own business and expected others to mind theirs. He kept a loaded shotgun behind his cash register and had no patience with nosy strangers, especially from north of the Mason-Dixon line. He was eighty-three; his granddaddy had fought in the Civil War. The only Yankee he'd ever met he liked all right was Elizabeth Stiles, and that was because she could shoot better than he did. "Good woman to have on your side in a fight," he had allowed.

A hellish one to have on the other side, Harlan had discovered. He had thought better of telling Danny he and Beth were divorced.

After a long shower in the bathroom he'd installed in a shed behind the cabin, Harlan put on shorts and a well-worn shirt and fixed himself a plate of sliced tomatoes from Danny's garden, fried white corn and country ham—a traditional Tennessee meal that reminded him of who he was. He sat on the porch and watched the sunset as he sipped gin and tonic and pondered his next move.

Should he take the coward's way out?

A phone call was all it would require. Do as the men who'd knocked him around had said and everything would be all right. He could return at once to a normal life. Beth would be safe. He expected she would be regardless of what he did. She knew nothing, after all, but he still wasn't free of that last, nagging doubt that maybe she was on his trail, after all.

I give in.

That was all he had to say. Three little words. He and the woman he had inadvertently dragged into this mess would be safe.

The men who had blackened his eyes and bruised his body would win.

So would the man who had ordered the thrashing.

Harlan chewed on an ice cube, listened to the crickets and thought. If anything happened to Beth, he wouldn't be able to live with himself. Putting himself in danger had been a deliberate choice on his part, even if the danger was more than he'd bargained for. It was a consequence of his own actions, something he accepted. Did he have a right to make that choice for Beth?

How could he live with himself if he abrogated every principle by which he operated?

Perhaps there was another way.

He started to throw the rest of his ice over the rail into the brush alongside his cabin, but stopped in mid-movement. He heard the snap of a twig underfoot and the crunch of gravel.

Crouching, he ignored the pain of his bruises and reached for the iron-handled poker he kept on the porch by the door, a prop of country life. It was the hour after dusk, when the shadows and sounds of the mountains were at their most mysterious. It would be easy, with the approaching night and his own frayed nerves, to mistake a rodent for an intruder.

"Whoa—yuck, I hate snakes!"

The disgust in the voice. Harlan gripped the poker hard, so he wouldn't start punching the nearest wall in frustration and bruise his hands as well.

There was no mistaking Beth Stiles when she was on a tear.

"Slither off into the woods where you belong," she muttered. "Though it doesn't surprise me to have a snake hanging out at this place. You guys know one of your own when you see one, don't you?"

Harlan leaned over the rail as Beth emerged from the brush, her hair all over the place and her skin unnaturally pale in the failing light. "You'd rather take on a grizzly bear than a harmless snake?"

"At least you can see a grizzly. A snake's done bit you and gone before you've seen it." She squinted up at him, then climbed the railing. In all the times she'd come to the cabin, Harlan couldn't remember her using the stairs. She hoisted herself over and landed squarely in front of him. "Well, Harlan, didn't you lead me on a merry chase?"

"Strangling you," he said, "would be too easy."

She nodded toward his poker. "Going to knock me on the head instead?"

His arms and fingers were so stiff that he almost had to pry the poker loose to set it down. The woman had always been impossible. Didn't he remember? Bossy, stubborn, know-it-all—a glorious pain in the ass. Nostalgia was to blame for the romantic spin he'd put on their years together.

"Think I was someone else sneaking up on you?" She was gloating, as if she had a right to be there, which she didn't. He'd let her know that soon enough, not that she'd care. "You should have known better. I'm the only person in the world who'd think to look for you here."

He hadn't seen Beth in *nine years*, and couldn't have anticipated that she would look for him in Coffee County. Yes, they'd spent countless nights here, nights filled with lovemaking and long, long conversations. That was long ago—a time she had made abundantly clear she was determined to forget. For all Beth knew, the cabin could have burned down, he could have sold it—or come to hate it, for all the memories of her it evoked.

"An unfortunate guess on your part," he told her.

"No way. I *knew*."

He eyed her dubiously. She was dead serious. Of course. Beth was always serious about what she *knew*. "You'll never change, Harlan. I realized that nine years ago when we split. You're like a wounded dog. You always come here to lick your wounds."

He subtly eased back against the porch wall, so she wouldn't guess what was going on in his mind or in his body. The memory of a steamy, love-filled night enveloped him. He could hear himself as a younger man, telling his wife what this place meant to him, why he would never give it up. Aside from their sexual compatibility, love for this isolated cabin in the country was the main thing they had had in common. When their marriage broke up, he had regretted having shared this part of himself with her. He'd vowed never to take a woman with him to Coffee County again. And never had. Beth had very nearly spoiled it for him, and he wouldn't risk that again.

Yet by coming here he had. His brain hadn't been working right since Beth had reentered his life, even peripherally, through Char and Stubborn Yankee.

"So we're both here." His voice sounded raspy even to him, betraying his tortured emotions. "Let's go inside away from the mosquitoes and decide what we're going to do about it."

He opened the screen door to let her go in first, then decided he'd better disclaim his actions immediately. "It's my house, and I'm being polite. I'd open the door for any of my guests."

"That's okay. I could hardly be mistaken for a damsel in distress tonight."

That was true enough. She looked like hell. *His* hell, though, as personal and familiar to him as his cracked ribs and bruises. They could never really be strangers. Because of that, they could never really be friends, either. The past hung over them when they were together, worked on their hormones, whittled away all they had become in their near decade apart. He was twenty-two again and captivated by this opinionated, beautiful Yankee, who—to his mother's dismay—had once shown an incompetent tree crew how to properly fell the dead elm in his parents' front yard. "That," Eleanor had told a neighbor about the woman in hard hat and leather chaps, wielding a chainsaw, "is my future daughter-in-law."

Harlan was no longer twenty-two, and Beth wasn't nineteen. She was thirty-four, he thirty-seven—both long past playing the kind of games they'd played with each other's hearts and minds a decade ago. Even if they weren't, this wasn't the time. He'd make that obvious to her and send her packing.

Her arm brushed his as she whirled past him and made his skin tingle. She glanced back at him, her lashes black against the smoky blue of her eyes. Her expression was serious, yet also evoked the hell-raising teenager who had once swept into his life and out again.

"We're doomed," she said, her own voice a little hoarse.

Harlan didn't dare touch her or smile. "I know."

BEING BACK in Coffee County, Beth fast discovered, wasn't like old times at all.

The cabin hadn't changed. There was the same wedding-ring quilt thrown over the same brass bed, the same sturdy pine trestle table, the same mismatched depression-ware. Still no curtains, still no cabinets. Dishes, pots and pans and canned food were all haphazardly arranged on open shelves, as they had been when Beth had first come to Coffee County fifteen years ago. Even the hooked rug in front of the stone fireplace was the same. They had bought it at a country fair one summer.

Yet if the cabin itself hadn't changed, everything else had—Harlan and herself, for certain. In the fading light of the humid August night she remembered who they had been. Kids, really, filled with unrealistic visions of the future, and even more unrealistic visions of their lives and of each other. Ahh, the past, Beth thought, unexpectedly saddened by her memories, not because of the wasted years with Harlan—she'd had to learn about men somehow—but because she felt so tired thinking about the dreams and plans she'd had at twenty.

These days her primary concern was getting hot water into her shack of a house, maintaining her running schedule, and pulling her weight at Mill Brook Post and Beam.

Or at least that had been the case until two days ago, when Jimmy Sessoms had called her Mrs. Rockwood and she'd discovered her ex-husband, not a rodent, in her attic. Now she was in Tennessee, dodging shadows of the past and hiding from old dreams.

Harlan poured her a glass of iced tea and handed it to her. He didn't sit down. Neither did she. She was too keyed up, too wired from the tension of not knowing if she'd find Harlan in Coffee County, and especially of not knowing if she was doing the right thing.

"We need to talk," she said.

He nodded. "I know."

"Adam—"

"Is ready to string us both up. I've talked to him," Harlan admitted.

"How much does he know?"

"Everything you do."

"Which is hardly anything," Beth said without bitterness.

"For damned good reason."

"Naturally. No need to get defensive."

"I'm not." He bit off his comment. She watched him squeeze his iced-tea glass. At least he looked better than he had the other night, when she'd had to peel him off her attic stairs. As she recalled, he'd always mended fast from his pummelings.

She drank her iced tea, continuing to watch him.

"You look beat."

His drawl was as clipped as it ever got, and she knew her cool was getting to him. If she were throwing things at him, he'd be fine. He'd treated her shabbily and knew it. Here she was, demanding justice. It clearly galled him, knowing that this time she had the upper hand.

"Take a shower, if you want. It's in the same place, plenty of towels." He swallowed the last of his tea, his eyes never leaving her. "Guess you'll have to stay the night. Suitcase in the car?"

"Just an overnight bag. I'll get it."

He gave her a long look, and she wondered if their shared past was troubling him, too. "Fine."

Those damned eyes of his! Her composure was slipping away. She felt hot and sweaty and sore—and on the edge of arousal, from that one, long, appraising stare. Beth had hoped her attraction to Harlan would have subsided with time, but it had apparently only lain dormant, like a powerful volcano.

"A shower probably would do me good. I won't be long." She stopped halfway to the door, turned, and thrust out one hand. "My car keys."

"What for?"

"You'll cut out on me while I'm in the shower, and I don't particularly want to chase you across Coffee County buck-naked. Folks would talk."

He smiled, moving toward her. "They'd just see your Vermont license plate and say that's a Yankee for you."

She was unmoved. "My keys."

He fished into his shorts pocket and dangled the keys in front of her. She snatched them away, feeling breathless. It had been a long, long time since anyone had challenged her the way Harlan did. "I didn't think you'd stay mad long enough to get this far," he said nonchalantly. "I thought you'd cool off at least by Pennsylvania and head back home." The spark went out of his eyes and the nonchalance vanished. "You should have, you know."

"That's what being around you does to me—destroys all my common sense. No wonder I can't think." She closed her fingers around her precious keys. "Ten minutes, tops. Be here when I get back."

She had gotten all the way out to the back porch when he called softly, in his slowest, richest drawl, "I could always steal the keys out of your shower."

"Try it, bub. See what it gets you."

Being naked within a hundred miles of Harlan would have had a detrimental effect on her nerves. Now she was showering in the very stall where they had made love on a number of all too memorable occasions.

She'd hung both sets of car keys on the hot-water faucet. If Harlan was going to sneak off, he'd have to head out on foot. At least he'd be easier to track down. Half expecting his sinewy hand to reach in at any moment and grab her keys, she got on with her shower. Efficiency counted now.

Keeping the water cooler than she ordinarily would have, Beth soaped up her hair and body. Slowly, almost against her will, she felt herself begin to relax. She was here. She had found him. Her guess had been on target. Now she'd get her car back and have a chance to insist on answers—if she wanted them. For all his many faults, Harlan was no fool. He would understand that he'd either deal with her fairly, or she'd trail after him like a hound after a weasel.

She closed her eyes and cranked up the hot water just a little, feeling it pelt against her skin and tired, taut muscles. She had done the right thing in coming. She knew she had. If the memories of their past had assaulted her psyche, she had the strength, the balance and self-assurance to endure it.

She sighed contentedly at the feel of the hot water in her hair.

She sensed his presence, not wanting to open her eyes to find out whether she was right. When Harlan's mouth closed over hers she knew she was right, but still didn't open her eyes.

His mouth was on hers, hot and wet, as real as the past had ever been in a decade of dreams. His tongue was inside her mouth, exploring, tasting.

Hot hands on her breasts, cupping, smoothing.

She moaned. Surely she'd gone mad, but it was a delicious madness.

She heard him groan and whisper her name, but it had been a long, long two days, and she was beyond exhaustion. Reality or fantasy, she was entitled to this indulgence. She thrust her hands against the shower stall and pressed hard to maintain her balance, to stop herself from reaching out for his hard, sleek body. She didn't want to grope in thin air, didn't want the fantasy to end.

Even with her eyes shut tight, tears streamed down her face. It had been so very long since her body had felt such yearning, such an exquisite ache.

Harlan Rockwood had always been real, never a simple fantasy.

His mouth descended lower, moved down her throat onto her breasts, licking, nipping, moving lower yet, until she felt the heat of his tongue between her legs. She cried out, not giving a damn who heard.

His tongue probed deeper and deeper. Beth realized her hips were swaying in rhythm. His mouth moved up her soaked abdomen to her breasts. He swept his arms around her waist and pulled her hips toward him.

Her pelvis touched him, and she finally opened her eyes. No apparition. No fantasy. He was here with her, a tougher man than she remembered, filled with pain and secrets that hovered behind his blackened eyes.

He whispered her name gently as he thrust into her, pulling her up and onto him as he moaned for her again and again. Ribs and bruises and all, he thrust harder, wildly, taking her with a hunger she had never experienced with him before. When the explosion came, it rocked them both, shattered them both. Nothing would ever be the same again.

Still, he tried reaching for the Chevrolet keys when it was over.

"Don't even think about it," she told him, breathless.

He left as silently as he'd come.

5

WHEN SHE RETURNED to the darkened cabin, Beth
wondered if she'd imagined the whole thing after all.
She spotted Harlan through the screen door, sitting
on the front steps in his shorts, an aspirin bottle and
drink at his side. She poured herself a glass of iced tea
and joined him.

At the squeak of the door, he turned and patted the
porch floor beside him. "Have a seat."

To be on the safe side, she sank into a wicker rocker.
He scooted around so that he was facing her, his back
pushed against the railing, his knees up. He looked his
old, languid self. Dressed in shorts and a sleeveless
top, Beth rocked steadily and sipped her tea. She
waited for him to initiate a conversation. If he started
to talk about what had happened in the shower, she
could always change the subject. She needed to find
out what he was thinking about. Did he intend to el-
bow her back to Vermont or give her the explanation
she deserved?

He drank some of his bourbon and picked up his
aspirin bottle, clutching it in one hand like a base-
ball. His gaze was focused on the label. Beth saw he
wasn't reading it. He was avoiding her eyes. "Beth—

you can't stay." His voice was tight, his words were clipped. "It's against my better judgment for you even to spend the night. There's no other choice, but you're out of here in the morning."

Since she'd thrown him out of her house, Beth had no grounds for complaining about him throwing her out of his cabin. She rocked harder.

"I'll see that your car gets back to you. I was a jerk for stealing it, but I felt so damned desperate...." His voice faded, and he released the aspirin bottle. "Maybe our being here together one last time was meant to be."

"Maybe." She stopped her rocking. "Look, Harlan, I never said I wanted to stay, and I certainly don't want to interfere in your affairs. I just want some idea of what the hell's going on."

He sighed. "You have all the ideas you're going to get. I shouldn't have gone to Vermont. I wasn't thinking straight. But that mistake ends here, now, tonight."

Undeterred, Beth asked, "Who beat you up?"

"Give it up, Beth."

"I figure it must have been at least two men. One to hold you and one to bash your face in."

Impatiently he ran one hand through the damp ends of his hair. It was a miracle he hadn't punctured a lung in the shower. She supposed his ribs weren't cracked, after all.

"I also figure," she persisted, "that you didn't accidentally run into them. Were they hired goons?"

He leaned back and silently stared up at the sky in obvious exasperation.

Beth resumed her slow rocking. "It stands to reason they were. They must have nailed you somewhere up north, otherwise you'd never have thought of coming to Millbrook, never mind have made it. So were they trying to make you do something, stop you from doing something, or both?"

"Don't make assumptions, Beth."

Something about his tone conjured up his past escapades. She remembered what an idealist he'd been. "So, Harlan, who put you on your white horse this time and told you to ride?"

He scowled at her. "I'm just be doing what I feel is right."

"The Rockwood sense of duty. Oh, Lordy. Haven't you ever heard of the police?"

His expression hardened. "The police are a dead end for now."

"Meaning there's insufficient evidence for arresting whoever hired those thugs who beat you up, to keep you, presumably, from scrounging around on your white horse."

"Stop." Despite his unwillingness to tell her a thing, there was a smile in his eyes. He climbed to his feet, walked toward her and took her hands into his. "Don't speculate, Beth. It won't do you any good. If nothing else, you'll end up imagining a worse mess for me than I'm already in."

"Then talk to me."

He pulled her to her feet. "Look at me, Beth." He moved closer, so she could see the slowly healing cuts and bruises on his ravaged face. There were dark, dark circles under his eyes. He didn't look as boyish or as idealistic as she remembered. "You'll head home in the morning."

"Is that an order?"

"A strong suggestion." He let her hands drop, brushed one cheek. "You're a special woman to me, Beth. You always will be. Now—you can have the bed. I'll sleep out here on the screened end of the porch."

"You don't have to. I mean, there's a couch...."

He smiled. "Too close to the bed. I tried that once. You'll have the bed, but it'll be cooler out here. A fair trade-off. Good night, Beth."

He wasn't going to budge. He didn't owe her an explanation. She had to admit that much. She started inside, but stopped at the door and looked back at him, standing in the shadows. "Harlan—no regrets, okay?"

He nodded. "Okay."

"Be careful and sleep well."

Inside, she listened to the crickets as she pulled the quilts off the brass bed, planning to sleep under a sheet in the humid heat. All the windows were opened. If Harlan tried anything in the night, she'd hear him.

Through the screen door he drawled, "Uh . . . Beth, there could be just one regret in all this."

She whirled around, intensely aware of his silhouette against the night. "What?"

"The silver lining is that you can't drive two cars north, so it's lucky you borrowed Julian's Rover. You can drive it back."

She hadn't considered the logistics of getting two Vermont vehicles back north. "What about the Chevy?"

"It can't make the trip."

"What do you mean?"

"I all but had to push it the last hundred miles. Beth, the Bel Air's a museum piece."

He'd always called her Chevy "the Bel Air," as if it made it something it wasn't. Either that, or he'd called it "that damned bomb of yours."

"What's wrong with it?" she asked.

He came through the door. "It won't run."

She sat on the edge of the bed. "A tune-up and an oil change and it'll be fine."

"I just put over a thousand hard miles on it. How long can a car last?"

"You'd better hope this one lasts several more thousand miles or what those creeps did to you will pale next to what I'll do!"

"Beth, the Bel Air's a goner."

He clearly relished his words. She snorted, "Now who's lacking sympathy?"

"For a *car*? A twenty-five-year-old car, to boot! You're damned right I have no sympathy! I'm standing here with cracked ribs and enough cuts and bruises to put most men in the hospital, and you're fretting about your car."

"My car has been in my life a hell of a lot longer than you have. If you can do what you just did in the shower, you're damned well on the mend."

He grinned at her, very sexily. "What *I* did in the shower, Beth? Seems to me you were a willing partner."

"I never did act normal in this place."

He sauntered out, as if he'd enjoyed telling her about her car, and had known it'd get her blood boiling. Was he just trying to divert her from figuring out what he was up to?

She sprang up and locked the door behind him, not that it made any difference. He could come through a window if he had a mind to. And the bathroom was inconveniently outside.

Still, there was nothing quite like flipping a lock to tell a man to go to hell.

AFTER AN UNCOMFORTABLE night on a wicker couch too short for him, Harlan awoke early and sore. As he awkwardly got to his feet, he smelled coffee brewing, country ham frying, and heard Beth humming.

It was a clear, warm, gorgeous morning in Coffee County. A day to go fishing and sit on the porch. He might have done just that, had it not been for one Elizabeth Stiles and his own sense of duty.

Wearing only his khaki shorts, he headed inside. Beth gave him a cheerfully suspicious smile from the stove, where she had two skillets going. "Good morning," she said, her blue eyes gleaming.

"Morning. What's that red stuff?"

"Fried tomatoes."

"Hell of a thing to do to a tomato."

"Southerners fry everything."

"Not tomatoes we don't. Only a stubborn Yankee'd fry a tomato."

She made a face at him and ordered him to make toast. He complied, wondering what she was up to. "Glad to be leaving?"

"In my own way. I did a lot of thinking last night— not much sleeping, I'm afraid. Anyway, I realize I must be giving you the wrong impression. I didn't follow you because I want to interfere with your life or even really care what you're doing."

He set the pine table next to the window, with its view of the stream. "You wanted your car back."

"Well, yes, of course. But it's more than that. Let's just call it intellectual curiosity. If I hurled myself back into your life after nine years, wouldn't you want to know why?"

"I would. In fact, I do."

"Do?" She looked momentarily startled. "Oh, Char's horse. All her idea, I'm afraid. I hit the ceiling when I found out she'd hooked up with you."

He filled two mugs with coffee. "You had nothing to do with it?"

"No. There's nothing nice, quiet and normal about you, Harlan, even if I'm the only person who knows it. I've always been able to see through that pristine Rockwood reputation of yours."

"But you knew Char had gone to Nashville instead of Lexington to make her fortune in horses. Weren't you even suspicious?"

"What Char did was none of my business."

"You had a tidy sum invested with her. I think you suspected we were in a deal together, but didn't want to know."

"Think what you want to think," she said loftily, dumping her fried tomatoes into a bowl, then arranging the slices of country ham on a plate. "Oh, I soaked the ham in water to remove some of the salt."

Harlan didn't know whether to thank her or gag. He brought the mugs and toast to the table, she, the ham and tomatoes, and they sat down opposite one another in the same chairs they'd used a decade ago. It might have been cozy, but wasn't. Harlan was too conscious of the bad night he'd passed, of his bruised body and how it had gotten that way, of everything the complex woman across from him had meant to him and still did.

"You're leaving after breakfast, I take it," he said, making his tone as conversational as possible. Elizabeth Stiles wasn't the sort of person easily ordered about.

She cut into her slice of ham. "I just got here."

Her comment was more a statement of fact than one of intent. She was trying to get him to say more than he should. Trying the fried tomatoes, which tasted mushy and rotten, he studied her. Her hair was sticking out everywhere, and she had dark, puffy circles under her eyes. She wasn't twenty anymore and had her own way of living, very different from his.

She sliced another bit of ham. He noticed the black grease in her cuticles. He glanced over at the sink and saw a cloth that looked suspiciously like one of the pricy, Belgian cotton towels he had ordered from Williams-Sonoma.

"You had a look at the Bel Air?" he asked, his tone neutral.

"Not 'the' Bel Air, *my* Bel Air. Yes, I had a look. There's nothing wrong with it. It isn't used to long distances," she said testily.

Harlan took no offense. She had a perfect right to be testy. He had disrupted the stability of her life and now threatened to leave her with a wrecked car and no answers. In her place, he would have been twice as miserable.

He said with equanimity, "No one knows that bomb of yours better than you do."

It was true. The Bel Air had been her off-to-college present to herself. It had served her well, largely due to her meticulous care. Harlan had heard her creep out of the cabin after dawn and assumed she'd had to take a look at her car. Without proper equipment she could only give it a cursory inspection. If she'd looked for wear and tear after the long journey south, he'd bet she hadn't looked for evidence of sabotage. In fact, he *was* betting on it. He'd dragged Beth Stiles as far as he was going to into the fetid swamp of his affairs. Now he was going to push her out, even if it had to be the hard way. It was a question of doing what had to be done. Not that Beth would share his view.

"It'll make it back to Vermont fine," she said.

"Good. Then take it, and I'll see to it Julian gets his Land Rover back."

She stirred her coffee very slowly, her intense gaze riveted on him. "It's not that simple."

He could feel his expression harden. "Yes, it is that simple."

"I want to know what you were doing up north." She set her spoon down, too gently for it not to have been a conscious effort. "I feel I have a right to know."

"Maybe you do, and maybe your being in Tennessee is my just desserts for having been a damned fool in coming to Millbrook. This is as far as it goes, Beth. Go home."

He got up from the table, his breakfast unfinished, and headed outside to the spot under the oak where he'd parked the Bel Air. He moved slowly and clumsily because he hurt like hell, still paying for the downright lunacy that had sent him into her shower.

"Harlan Rockwood." Her voice was cool and stubborn as she followed him. "I didn't drive a thousand miles for you to shoo me off. I'm not trying to be unreasonable. The fact is, I intend to stick to you like a bee on a rosebud until you tell me what's going on."

"Potato beetle," he said. He saw the faint sheen of perspiration on her upper lip and the effects of the humidity on her wild hair, and he knew—promised himself—that he would make love to her again one day. Not today. But soon.

She frowned. "What?"

"A potato beetle is a bigger pest to a rosebud than a bee."

"I'd rather be a bee, thank you. It was a bad analogy. You're no rose. Now quit trying to distract me. Harlan, what are you doing?"

"Sticking my hand in your pocket." He could have lingered there, next to the warmth of her skin, but didn't. Instead he withdrew the keys to the Bel Air.

She gave him her deadliest look, one that would have stopped anyone else cold. One didn't ordinarily trifle with a woman who knew her chainsaws. "Don't you dare try to run off on me. I'll jump in the Rover and be on your tail before you're out to the main road."

"I'm not going anywhere." He left the door open as he slid behind the wheel and stuck the key into the ignition. "You are."

"You don't tell me what to do, Harlan Rockwood."

"All right, I won't. I'll tell you what *I'll* do if you don't get in this damned car of yours and head home. I figure I have three choices. One, I call your brothers and have *them* come fetch you."

She sniffed. "I am not a thirteen-year-old runaway."

"No, but how do you think Julian feels about you sneaking off in the dead of night with his Land Rover?"

Her look grew even deadlier. "Don't come between me and my brothers."

"If I give them the word, they'll be down here in a flash, with a straitjacket, if need be. I don't have the same history with them as I do with you. They know when it's time to back off."

She said nothing, but he could see the doubt in her eyes, behind the anger. He climbed out of the car. "Or, two, I call a certain local law enforcement official I know who hasn't reconciled himself to the defeat of the confederacy. Imagine what he'd do if I told him I had me a Yankee trespasser."

"I am not amused."

"Or, three..." He backed her against the side of the car and placed his hands on the hood, pinning her between his arms. "Three, we lock ourselves in my cabin and make love until I really do puncture a lung, or you realize the only option you have is to give up. I'm sorry I involved you, Beth, but I don't owe you anything, except maybe flowers when you have to bury your Bel Air."

Her eyebrows drew together as she examined him, and he knew he was winning—or at least penetrating that Yankee will of hers.

She slid under his arm and took a couple of steps out of his reach. "What you're saying is that you used me."

"That's a harsh view. I look upon it as having taken refuge with an old friend in an hour of profound need. A mistake, perhaps, not a deliberate act of cruelty." He found himself smiling as he spoke. "A rerun of one of our old arguments, isn't it? I never mean to hurt you, but always do."

"Don't flatter yourself. I'm not hurt, Harlan. I'd have to care about you a lot more than I do for you to be able to hurt me."

Her old defense—*I don't care, so how can I be hurt?* He resisted the temptation to touch her, to hold her. "Then why do you want to know what kind of mess I'm in, if you don't care?"

"Okay—you win. I'm not one to stick around where I'm not wanted, and if you're in a mess, I guess it's for you to decide what to do about it. Now if you don't mind, all this yammering's wasting gas. I'll grab my suitcase and be gone."

He couldn't hide his astonishment.

She grinned at him. "None of your three options is palatable to me. Besides, you're absolutely right. I don't need to know what you're up to. I need to get home, get back to my animals and my work and prove to my brothers that you could have saved yourself a whole lot of trouble if you'd stolen one of their cars instead of mine. You will get Julian's Rover back to him?"

"Promise."

"Don't try to substitute another. He's just gotten this one broken in."

"I understand the Stiles's attachment to their vehicles."

She leaned forward and kissed him lightly on the mouth. It was all he could do to stop himself from hauling her back inside to his brass bed. *Their* bed. He couldn't believe she was going.

"Take care of yourself, Beth." This was it, he thought. She was going. Maybe she really didn't care about him. "Drive carefully."

"Yeah. If you need me..." She sighed, and he could see her struggling with herself. Then she blundered on. "If you need me, you know where to find me. No matter how impossible we are together, I'd never turn you away."

She fetched her own suitcase, and Harlan watched and waved as she backed the old Bel Air onto the dirt road. She looked every bit the wild girl who'd had no idea, so long ago, how a simple car could stir up the Rockwood world. Her Chevy ran, got decent mileage, and she could do her own tune-ups. That it was ugly as sin, old even then, and was perceived, when she continued to hang onto it after "becoming a Rockwood," as an affront, had been completely beyond her. It had been that adherence to her own values, that absolute sense of what she was about, right or wrong, that had both appealed to him and exasperated him. After a year he'd had enough of her damned car, too. Without even a glance back, she popped the Bel Air into second and roared off.

For a moment Harlan didn't move. He tried to tell himself it was for the best, that his feelings of aloneness and defeat would pass. At least he was no longer torn between pushing her away and pulling her toward him. She was gone, for another nine years, perhaps even forever.

He swallowed hard, felt tears spring to his eyes, and willed it not to be so. For a while, yes. Not forever. He had made a promise to himself, hadn't he?

He clenched his fists at his sides. "She didn't look back. Not even a glance." Not even after what had happened last night in the shower. True, he had gone to her, but she could have thrown a bar of soap at him or told him to march. She hadn't. She had wanted him as much as he had wanted her.

She could have blown him a kiss, waved, or even stuck out her tongue. Something.

"Oh, hell."

He kicked the sandy driveway and felt a stab of pain in his abdomen for his effort. Whatever Beth was up to, she wasn't going quietly back to Vermont. He momentarily considered following her in the Land-Rover, deciding it would only prompt her to come up with another plan. Better to go back about his business, with extreme caution.

Right now he needed coffee and a chance to clear his head.

He finished his breakfast, scraped the slimy tomatoes into the compost, and after his third cup of coffee was thinking straight again.

He had to forget the stupid elation he'd felt at the prospect that Beth hadn't come after him just for that damned bomb of hers. Common sense—common *decency*—told him this wasn't the time to egg Beth Stiles on, nor the time to confront his feelings about her or force her to face up to her feelings about him. What held true Friday morning in Vermont, when he'd left her sleeping amidst her quilts and critters, held true now.

He couldn't put her in the same danger he'd put himself.

First things first, he told himself. First, his predicament with the *gentlemen* who wanted him silent and acquiescent. Then Beth.

He knew that wouldn't fit into her view of the world at all. She wasn't someone who took too well to being compartmentalized or put on hold.

"Too bad, darlin'. No way will I be responsible for anything happening to you."

Unfortunately, the chances that Beth had gone merrily on her way were somewhere between slim and none. It wasn't her style to butt out—so it was just as well he'd anticipated as much, sometime before dawn, and had taken appropriate measures to stall her.

HOT AND CURSING, Beth pulled the limping Chevy onto the side of the deserted country road and slammed the door when she leaped out. Even for Coffee County, it was a boiling morning. Her shirt stuck to her back. She'd kicked off her shoes and driven barefoot. Her plan had been to double back, avoiding the main roads, and spy on her ex-husband. Her right rear tire, however, had gone flat, probably picking up one of the sharp stones in the road.

She squatted to have a look.

"That *snake!*"

A stone wasn't at fault. A key had been wedged under her tire, so that when she drove off, it would cause a puncture.

Sabotage, plain and simple.

Well, at least she knew how to change a tire. It wouldn't be a pleasant job in the stifling heat, but she'd get it done. Warning herself that fury would only make her hotter, she gritted her teeth and opened the trunk.

Her spare tire was gone.

Fifteen minutes ago she had had her doubts about what she was doing. She had considered the possibility that she had turned Harlan's mess into an obsession, had entertained the idea of being sensible and heading home. Why keep sticking her nose in where it wasn't wanted?

That had been fifteen minutes ago, before her tire blew, before she'd found the key, before she'd discovered she had no spare tire.

Now she had no doubts.

She snatched an old Boston Red Sox cap from her trunk, banged the trunk shut and put the cap upon her sweaty curls. She didn't want to collapse from heat exhaustion, in case Harlan Rockwood had informed all of Coffee County to leave her in a ditch for the snakes if they happened upon her.

Pacing herself, she started walking toward town.

HARLAN DUMPED his leather overnight case onto the floor in front of the Land-Rover's passenger seat. Beth had left him with about an eighth of a tank of gas. Keeping an eye out for her notorious car, he rumbled into town. He didn't see the Bel Air, but that was all right. He knew she was out there. The woman was implacable.

He stopped at the general store and filled his gas tank, not surprised to discover that Danny had heard Harlan's "wife" was in town. "Ain't seen her hereabouts in a while," Danny said.

"She hasn't changed," was the only response Harlan could come up with.

He used the pay phone at the back of the store to call Julian Stiles, explaining about Beth and the flat tire she had no doubt encountered.

"You don't think she'll just fix the tire and come straight home?" Julian asked.

"Not a chance."

There was a pause at Julian's end of the line. "Harlan, I don't want to interfere, but maybe keeping all of us in the dark isn't such a good idea."

Harlan sighed grimly. "The way I see it, I don't have a choice. I'll get your Rover back to you as soon as I can. You can collect your sister whenever you want."

Julian grunted. "Think I'll let her cool down first."

"Probably not a bad idea." Harlan could just imagine the names she'd called him when she'd discovered her spare tire was missing. "Don't worry. She won't get out of Coffee County."

Hanging up, Harlan made another call, this one to New York City.

"Thought you chickened out," Saul Rabinowitz of the *Manhattan Chronicle* said.

"No."

"What gives, then? We had a date for Tuesday afternoon and you were a no-show. I know you rich folks have your priorities, but I don't play games."

"I know you don't. I'm sorry I didn't call. I'd like to reschedule, if you're still willing."

Harlan knew Saul's hesitation was pure theatrics—an attempt at punishment. He was too sharp a reporter, too scrupulous, too competitive to let martyrdom ruin a potential story.

"When?" Saul asked.

"Today's Sunday.... I'll need a day or two to regroup."

"You've had more than day or two. Meet me tonight, eight o'clock, same place."

The Upper West Side of Manhattan. "Can't."

"Rockwood, I don't let anyone jerk me around."

"I'm a thousand miles away."

"So? You can afford to hire a private jet if you need to. Be here, or the deal's off."

"What deal? I'm not getting anything out of this." *Aside from a few cracked ribs and an outraged ex-wife.*

"The hell you aren't. You're getting my time."

Harlan reminded himself that he didn't have to like Saul Rabinowitz, although he had a feeling he would, if they ever managed to meet. He appreciated people who didn't beat around the bush.

"Let me ask you this," Harlan said, abandoning the subject of rescheduling for the moment. "Has anyone come to see you about me?"

Saul answered without hesitation. "No. *I* kept my promise to keep mum about our meeting. Don't want to look like a damned fool, if you turn out to be a paranoid jerk, you know—which I don't mind telling you is looking more and more like the case."

"I understand."

"Yeah. Either you're a paranoid rich boy or something really is up. Someone tried to scare you off our meeting, huh?"

"No one knows I'm meeting with you."

"They know you're rat-finking to someone."

"Rat-finking" wasn't the word Harlan would have chosen but he let it slide. "I'm in a delicate position."

"How bad they hurt you?"

"No broken bones or stitches."

"Ouch, ouch." Saul was obviously delighted. "I take it you want me to come to you?"

"Yes." Harlan already had his plan worked out. "The Parthenon, noon on Tuesday."

"I've got to go to *Greece?*"

"Nashville," Harlan said. "Centennial Park, near Vanderbilt University. The Parthenon's a museum. We'll do this on my turf."

"So if anybody fries, it'll be me. Thanks a lot."

"You game?"

"Yeah, what the hell. I think I read about this Parthenon in the fifth grade. I'll find you. I blend into a crowd a hell of a lot better than you do."

"You don't know what I look like."

"Make a bet? A rich boy doesn't call me out of the blue and arrange a powwow and I don't check him out. I probably know more about you than you do yourself. You just be at this Parthenon. I'll find you."

Saul hung up, and Harlan reluctantly replaced the receiver. Skulduggery wasn't his thing. It would have been easy to resume his normal schedule and forever remain a no-show, a source of irritation in Saul Rabinowitz's life. Never mind that his bruised ribs were a partial reward for his refusal to name the reporter whom he'd intended to meet. What he was doing wasn't simply a matter of revenge. It was primarily a question of honor—something his ex-wife no doubt would find quaintly Old South.

As if he wasn't sweating enough, when he turned from the telephone he almost knocked her over. There she was, standing squarely, breathing rapidly, arms crossed over her chest, her hair matted to her forehead and temples. Her clothes were drenched with perspiration.

He gave her a guiltless grin. "Thought you were long gone."

"Thought I was stuck out in the woods with snakes and bears is what you thought."

She was clearly in a foul mood. "What'd you do, try to spy on me?"

The flash in her blue eyes told him that was exactly what she'd done. "You sabotaged my car."

"You have proof?"

"A BMW key in my tire's all the proof I need."

"A BMW key? I must have lost it on the driveway. I wondered what happened to it."

"I'll bet. You knew I'd never make it out of the county. You *planned* it that way."

"Discretion is the better part of valor. Would you like a soda?"

"I'll be fine, no thanks to you."

She would, too. He'd assumed he'd be on his way long before she could catch up with him. If he'd remembered her obsession with fitness, he might have postponed his phone calls.

"Who were you talking to on the phone?" she demanded.

"Your brother Julian. He's agreed to lend me his Rover for a few days."

"You tell him you stranded me in Coffee County?"

Beth took his silence for confirmation. "Well, you can call him back and tell him I'm not stranded anymore. I'm going with you."

"No, Beth," Harlan said, "you're not."

"Give it up, Harlan. I am."

"I thought you'd agreed to go. . . ."

Not even the slightest twinge of guilt registered on her hot, beautiful face. "What's good for the goose is good for the gander, Rockwood."

"This time I was one step ahead of you."

"'Was' is right. Now we're even."

"Not quite. Danny?"

"What're you calling him for? You know I make him nervous."

His soft paunch preceding him, Danny walked over and calmly observed Harlan, whose family he'd known for over fifty years. Harlan spun Beth around and pushed her toward his old friend.

"Danny, she's going to get herself in a heap of trouble if she follows me. Keep her here, all right? One of her brothers'll be down for her soon."

Beth turned red. "I'll have you charged with kidnapping."

"Try it," Harlan told her. "Danny's son is the local sheriff."

He had no idea if that was true or not, but knew that Danny wouldn't contradict him.

"Stick her in the smokehouse or something. I owe you one."

"You don't owe me nothing," Danny said. "Glad to help."

Harlan kissed Beth hard on the mouth. She did not kiss him back. He was counting on her sense of fair play not to kick an old man in the shins and bolt.

He didn't relax, however, until he had reached the interstate, heading west into Nashville, no 1965 Chevrolet Bel Air in his rearview mirror.

BETH REMAINED COMPOSED after Harlan departed rural Coffee County in her brother's Land-Rover. She smiled when she heard him grind the gears of Julian's Rover, gleefully imagining what his backside and bruised body would feel like after a couple of hours of bouncing around. He had definitely tried to put one over on her in a way that struck her as both arrogant and annoying. The prospect of Adam or Julian flying to Tennessee to fetch their little sister didn't sit well with her at all.

But she wasn't as angry as she might have been simply because she had Harlan this time.

If only she knew why she'd even bothered. He got her blood boiling, to be sure, leaving her with a flat tire and an elderly man who'd love to nail him a Yankee. But her motives for not throwing in the towel and heading back home had nothing to do with her car. She had her car. What they had to do with she didn't want to know right now. She had work to do.

"I need to make a phone call," she told Danny.

The old man mulled over her request a moment. "Guess it won't do any harm."

He directed her to the pay phone Harlan had used. She dialed Taylor and Eleanor Rockwood's residence. Eleanor answered.

Beth turned her back to Danny. "Mrs. Rockwood, it's Beth Stiles. I'm calling to find out if you've heard from Harlan."

"Yes, thank heaven. He called not long ago. This has all been the most embarrassing misunderstanding. I'm very sorry to have worried you, Elizabeth."

"Oh, I wasn't worried. You know Harlan. Anyway, does this mean you've called off Jimmy Sessoms?"

"Well . . . no, not yet. I will, as soon as he makes contact with me." Eleanor sounded tentative, even self-conscious. "Harlan had forgotten our brunch and gone fishing. He has had a great deal on his mind and was due for a break. He was never even in Vermont."

Beth knew her own family would have stuck up for her in the same way Eleanor Rockwood was sticking up for her son. Or didn't she have any idea Harlan was lying?

"When are you expecting Harlan back?" Beth asked casually.

She heard Eleanor hesitate. "Elizabeth—Beth, I know you'll understand I'm in an awkward position. If Harlan would like to speak with you, I'm sure he will. Now if you'll excuse me, I have an appointment."

"Of course."

Beth hung up, wondering why she'd bothered to call. To see if Eleanor knew more than she did? If he'd confided in her? Stupid. Eleanor was right. If Harlan wanted to tell his ex-wife anything, he would.

He'd already made damned clear that wasn't what he had in mind.

She turned to Danny. "You know how to change a tire on a 1965 Chevrolet?"

"I sure do, ma'am. They don't build cars like they used to."

She smiled her best smile. "They sure don't. Harlan tell you I have a problem with mine?"

Danny was stone-faced.

"You could save my brother a lot of trouble if you could fix it before he gets here."

Of course, she could fix it herself. She wasn't going to tell Danny that.

He rubbed his ample chin. "Pretty handy with cars yourself, I recall."

"I used to be," she said, aware that for all his prejudices, Danny was no fool.

"You're a handful, Mrs. Rockwood. I don't envy Mr. Rockwood one smidge."

Beth considered Danny's comment highly sexist, but resisted the temptation to let him have it. He took her out to her disabled car in his tow truck, admired the old Chevy, and told her more about the good old days while he had a look.

"Not too promising, ma'am, but I guess you already know that. You shouldn't keep running on a flat. Good way to wreck the rim."

Beth knew that, but Harlan had driven her to do even worse in the past. She smiled casually at the old man. Danny went to work, and she observed him do exactly what she'd have done to get the Chevy back onto the road.

"I'll send someone back for it," he offered.

"That's not necessary. I'll drive."

"Now, Mrs. Rockwood, you and I both know if I let you in that car, you're just going to chase off after your husband when he doesn't want you pestering him."

The man was cannier than she'd bargained for. "And you know you're over eighty," she said sweetly, "and I could muscle my way past you if I had a mind to."

To her surprise, he didn't take offense. Instead he shook his head, as if he couldn't believe he'd gotten roped into keeping an eye on this Yankee viper. "You haven't changed."

"Tell you what. I can drive your tow truck and you can drive my Bel Air." Lord, she was starting to sound like Harlan.

"Likely enough, then, I'm out of a truck."

Beth sighed. "Danny, Harlan's in over his head this time. I know he is."

"If he wanted your help—"

"He'd never ask for it, and you know it. Now, wouldn't you want me on your side in a fight?"

"Hate for you to be on the other side, for sure."

"Please understand, I'd never do anything that would endanger Harlan."

Danny twisted his mouth to one side. "It's endangering you I think he's fretting over."

"Without cause."

"I reckon you're right about that, but I promised Mr. Rockwood I'd look after you."

"Then who's going to look after him?"

"You're going to sneak off no matter what I say, aren't you? Truth to tell, ma'am, he told me not to worry much if you did, as you won't be able to find him anyhow."

The rat. Beth kept her face expresionless and shrugged. "I guess you're right about that. At least I can try to help him."

"Well," Danny said with a heavy sigh, "I've got too much work to do to chase after a Yankee who doesn't have the good sense to do what her man asks her to do. You'll do what you do, I reckon."

Beth grinned. "I reckon I will. You're not making me feel guilty."

Wise, old eyes looked at her. "Didn't expect I would."

He had the good grace to wish her well when she headed off, only refusing to lie for her if Harlan checked in.

"I'd as soon hold onto an angry rattlesnake as you," were his parting words.

Danny would have hog-tied her before letting her go if he'd realized she'd listened in on Harlan's conversation and knew precisely where her ex-husband was headed.

If not before, she'd see that scheming rascal and the person who was meeting him at the Parthenon in downtown Nashville at noon on Tuesday.

6

By ten o'clock Tuesday morning, Harlan had had two nights and one full day to regain his strength. Dressed in an old pair of jeans and a black T-shirt he'd had at the cabin in Coffee County, he walked along a shady Nashville street.

Beth was up to something. There hadn't been a word from her since he'd turned her over to Danny. He had toyed with the idea of calling the country store in Coffee County or Mill Brook Post and Beam. He had resisted, concluding that anything he said or did would only egg Beth on. Best to say and do nothing.

All the same, he doubted she'd gone quietly back to home and job. He had no grounds for his suspicions. He hadn't heard from her or the Stiles clan or read in the papers that she was in trouble. From the room he'd taken at a down-and-out Nashville hotel, he checked the messages on his answering machine.

Not a word from or about his ex-wife.

His suspicions arose from instinct. He knew her. Despite all her complaints about him, Beth herself wasn't one to back off from trouble. She was a hothead who'd never been content to sit on the sidelines.

He suspected she was in hiding herself, waiting for him to resurface.

"She doesn't know anything."

Lord, he thought. Something about Beth always managed to get him talking to himself.

He stopped dead. The heat, the stress. He had to be seeing things.

"No."

He moved slowly toward the curb, put out his hand toward the apparition. The metal under his fingertips was smooth and warm and very real. A 1965 Chevrolet Bel Air. Sea green. It was parked at an angle, a half block down from the building where Beth Stiles and Harlan Rockwood had spent their first months of marriage.

Harlan didn't bother checking for the Vermont plates. There could only be one 1965 Chevrolet Bel Air outside junkyards and collectors' fleets.

The lunatic was going to crash his meeting with Saul Rabinowitz.

"How?" Harlan looked for something to kick. "How did she find out?"

He clenched his hands into tight fists and smashed one down onto the roof of her eyesore of a car.

"The nosy little pain in the neck eavesdropped. Damn!"

He remembered turning around at Danny's and finding her standing there, looking smug. He'd assumed she wouldn't have been able to resist interrogating him if she'd overheard his conversation with Saul. What arrogance on his part. What *stupidity*. She had damned well learned to play her cards close to her chest.

"I should never underestimate that woman."

Beth swung around the corner in bright orange shorts, a white T-shirt and sneakers. She walked briskly lost in her own thoughts and memories. Nashville was filled with them. Back in Vermont she could escape the tangible reminders of Harlan and their years together. Out of sight, out of mind.

She didn't see Harlan until she almost bumped into him.

"You!" she exclaimed, and bolted.

"Hey!"

He lunged after her. With long, loping strides, he trailed her around the corner, then cranked up his pace and caught up with her when she began to fade in the August heat. He reached out, grabbed her by the forearm, and spun her around in a whirl of sweaty hair and curses.

She snatched her arm free. "If I could *breathe* you'd never have caught up with me."

"You never did like to lose." Harlan saw her chest heaving as she gulped for air in the stifling humidity. He sighed. "Beth—dammit, what do I have to do to get through to you? I don't want you here."

She caught her breath. "So what?"

"So you're not so different from me as you'd like to believe." He noticed his teeth were clenched. She had managed to get to him again. "In my own way, Beth, I'm just as driven and absorbed as you are. I wouldn't forget that if I were you."

"Calling me driven isn't going to stop me."

"Let's say you're independent-minded and leave it at that."

She scowled at him, looking every bit the stubborn Yankee she was. If only her eyes weren't so damned blue. "I know you're meeting Saul Rabinowitz. He's an investigative reporter for the *Manhattan Chronicle*. Took me a day, but I found out."

Harlan felt chilled. "Beth, how did you find out? Did you talk to anyone?"

"I'm not an idiot, Harlan. I knew he was probably from New York, and gathered whoever used you for a hockey puck would gladly do the same to him, if given the chance. I watch TV. I faked a story and a name and got the info I wanted, without giving away a thing I know—which is damned little."

"Ever hear of minding your own business?"

She was unimpressed. "You made yourself my business when you snuck into my attic."

"Well, I'm unmaking myself your business right now."

"Dream on, Rockwood. You don't tell me what to do."

He had never met anyone so combative, so sure her way was the only way. Then her expression softened, and when she squinted, he saw the faint lines at the corners of her eyes and was poignantly aware of the passage of time.

"Beth. Oh, Beth. I've caused you enough misery." He touched her cheek, brushed at a sweaty strand of hair that clung to her temple. "I can't cause you more."

"Then talk to me, Harlan. You know I'm not going to give up until I have some answers." She fastened her intense blue eyes upon him. "You're right. I've had two days to think, and you don't owe me an explanation."

He shook his head. "No, I do. I came to your house, stole your car, turned your life upside down. Tell me, if I hadn't been up in your attic, what would you have done about Jimmy Sessoms?"

"I like to think I'd have forgotten him by the next morning. That's probably wishful thinking. Otherwise I wouldn't have called your parents. To be honest, I'd have done everything I could to track you down myself. It's not a matter of owing you or even of curiosity, but of doing what I feel is right. I don't like to walk away when the going gets tough." She was silent a moment, then said, "I did that nine years ago."

"Beth . . ."

"No, don't. It's not easy being here, Harlan. Don't make it harder."

He placed his hand gently on her forearm. "I've got time. Let's find a place and get something to drink."

BETH ORDERED iced coffee. She sank against the wooden back of the booth in a dark, quiet corner of the tavern—the tavern where she and Harlan used to come as students for grilled hamburgers and frosty beers. Later on they'd fought there, and she'd come to feel like a Yankee outsider who didn't like grits and complained about the heat as early as May. Everyone had known her as Harlan's wife, a Rockwood. Her identity had begun slipping away. She'd blamed Harlan, because he was her husband, a Rockwood, a southerner, a part of this world—his world. And they lived in his world. If there'd been a way to compromise, she hadn't been able to discover it, and neither had he. First he'd have had to come to terms with who he was, a hundred-percent Rockwood, not the rebel he'd believed himself to be. *Just be yourself*, he'd told her, as if it were easy, as if oppressive family pressures didn't exist.

"I haven't come in here in years." He gazed around the old tavern, almost empty over an hour before lunch. Beth realized how much more at peace with himself he was now. As she was herself. Why were they risking the stability they'd created in their lives? Harlan continued, "Menu's the same, though."

"Prices are higher. Lord, this place makes me feel old."

Harlan laughed. "I know what you mean. Time marches along, doesn't it?"

"And people grow up." A chunky waitress delivered their iced coffees. Beth took a sip, relishing the cold liquid in her parched mouth. She couldn't resist adding, "Some of us, anyway."

Unabashed, he grinned. "Beth, I want you to know I haven't been in a fight since we split. If I had, maybe I'd have handled myself better in this one. The fights I had while we were married were legitimate. I was into boxing. Sparring isn't the same as a bar fight."

She shrugged. It was an old argument. "A black eye is a black eye."

"It's not. With a legitimate opponent there are rules. You know he's not going to kill you."

"Not intentionally, anyhow. Don't pretend you weren't in your share of brawls."

"My rebellious phase," he said philosophically. "I thought you liked me best when I was rebelling against being a Rockwood."

"I liked you best when you were just being yourself. That's water over the dam, as they say. I don't want to get bogged down rehashing the past. Whatever went wrong between us went wrong. So be it. Tell me about your fight in New York."

"It wasn't a fight. It was a beating. One man held me down, while . . ."

"Only one?"

"He was big. The other pounded me wherever he could land a punch."

Harlan saw Beth wince. "Let's just say they made their point."

"Which was?"

He bought himself a few extra minutes by drinking his coffee and chewing on a piece of ice. Neither the passage of time nor maturity had made Harlan enjoy telling other people his business any more than he had nine years ago.

"They knew I was meeting a reporter."

"Saul Rabinowitz."

Harlan settled back against the booth and didn't meet Beth's eye. "They wanted me to cancel and to give them his name. We 'compromised.' They beat me up so badly I couldn't make my appointment. I also was unconscious and couldn't give them Saul's name. When I came to, I knew I needed to regroup. So I headed to Vermont. It was close, I knew you were there." He shrugged, still bewildered by what had propelled him northward. "I figured it was the last place anyone would look for me."

"Saul didn't know what had happened?"

"He thought I'd chickened out. Figured I was a rich boy trying to stir up trouble—a tempest in a teapot, he said. He didn't have much faith in what I could tell him, yet he didn't mind chasing down a lead. For all I know, he's cut his losses and won't show today."

"You're protecting him?"

"As much as I can. I don't want anyone getting hurt or, God forbid, killed over something I insist on pursuing."

"I see." Beth drank more iced coffee, felt less certain of herself and her mission. Had *she* endangered Harlan or Saul with her insistence on getting answers? "What hornet's nest did you stir up?"

Harlan looked away, Beth sensed the concern and pain he was feeling. This wasn't a game to him. "A bigger one than I imagined, apparently. You recall the horse swindle that almost ruined Char?"

Did she ever. "She lost everything and ended up living in a tent for a while, blaming you for having swindled her."

Harlan managed a weak smile. "You didn't rise to my defense?"

"Not a chance. When I found out what had happened, or what Char *thought* had happened, I would have helped her string you up. Never mind that you were ultimately proved innocent. Trouble has a way of finding you, Harlan."

He didn't argue that point. "Initially I blamed an unscrupulous horse trainer for the whole mess. He'd switched my yearling for a dead ringer, who was a dud. I could have found out sooner if I'd had any inkling what was going on. I assumed the trainer had sold my yearling to an unsuspecting buyer overseas. I launched my own investigation of the incident. Now I'm convinced the buyer wasn't so unsuspecting."

"He put the trainer up to the switch?"

"Precisely."

"Can't you get the law after him?"

"Would it were so easy. He's a foreigner and seldom sets foot in the States. Right now I'm concentrating on presenting evidence of his irregularities to Saul. I'll let him write an article and see how the cookie crumbles, so to speak. I'm hoping at least to get this guy barred from racing, if not thrown in jail. I had no idea he was capable of violence. I have a feeling horse swindles are the least of his dirty dealings."

Beth had the same feeling. "Aren't you worried about libel?"

"There's no reckless disregard for the truth here and no falsehoods. That's why I went to Saul. He's the best."

"So you'll be his background source."

"Yes."

"How'd the bad guys find out you were onto them?"

"I'm not a pro, Beth. I tipped them off somehow. Perhaps I should have hired a P.I. I didn't know if I was barking in the wind or really onto something."

"And more fun to do your own dirty work."

"More satisfying, maybe. I wouldn't say fun." He studied her with hooded eyes. "Word got back to him. It doesn't matter how. He tried to stop me."

Beth turned away from his probing gaze. "You're not the kind of rich boy who backs off after getting his nose bloodied. No, you came back for more."

"In my place, what would you do?"

She looked at him for a long time, exhausted by two near sleepless nights on the road, by being kept awake wondering, and by the onslaught of memories. Then she declared, "I'd meet with Saul Rabinowitz."

THE PARTHENON in Nashville, Tennessee, an exact replica of the original in Athens, Greece, was located in picturesque Centennial Park, where Harlan and Beth had spent countless evenings strolling hand in hand. Now she pushed her memories aside and observed her ex-husband from the edge of a parking lot. Even in his shabby clothes, he looked as straight-backed and confident as ever.

Without so much as a glance over his shoulder, he disappeared into the cavernous interior of the art museum, an unusual location for a clandestine meeting with an investigative reporter.

Since Beth had crossed the Mason-Dixon line, heading south, she had been enveloped in nostalgia. Again and again, she'd recalled Harlan as he had been. Today, for the first time, she was aware of seeing him as he was now. He had carved out a place for himself in the long, daunting Rockwood tradition, as she had in the tradition of the Stiles family. He could no more not be a Rockwood than she could be anything but a Stiles. It was so damned simple—and sad. He was comfortable with who he was, and she was comfort-ble with who she was. Did that mean they couldn't be anything more than occasional lovers?

She squinted in the bright, hazy sunshine. Was Saul Rabinowitz already inside the Parthenon, waiting for Harlan?

"Harlan, Harlan," she murmured. His name felt good on her lips. If she could come out of this mess feeling peaceful when she thought about him, then her time hadn't been wasted and her emotions rubbed raw without reason. He was handsome, honorable, and more sensible than he had ever been. Yesterday, to pass the time, she had driven past the Rockwood estate and past his own immense Greek Revival house on the Cumberland River. He was as much a part of the central Tennessee basin as were its rolling hills and sleepy rivers.

He was content to be in Tennessee.

Well, she was content in Vermont.

Why was she feeling so depressed, then?

Harlan didn't need her. She should be relieved and go on with her own life. Get back to her pets and on with fixing up old Louie's place.

She had agreed to let Harlan meet Saul in peace. It was all he had asked of her. He had promised nothing himself. He hadn't offered to see her afterward and tell her what had happened. He hadn't suggested they ride off to Vermont together and wait for the dust to settle. Hadn't mentioned the future beyond noon and Saul. She had refused to ask him what he thought she should do. What she should do was her own decision.

She had contemplated waiting in the parking lot, keeping an eye on the Parthenon until Harlan emerged, with or without Saul. She wanted this business resolved, or wanted some sign that her ex-husband wasn't finished with her.

It appeared he was.

His presence in her attic in Vermont had been what he'd said it was: a choice born of necessity. A place to hide until his head cleared.

She climbed into her car, shut the door hard, turned the key and backed out, heading east and then north. Before long she'd be home.

HARLAN SENSED that this time Beth was gone. He'd spotted her Bel Air in the parking lot and known she was watching him, if not watching out for him. He assumed she was making up her mind about what she should do. Stay? Leave? Meddle? She was no good at playing the supportive helpmate. Supportive she could be, but never someone who said things just to make someone feel good. With Beth, you got what you asked for.

What had he asked for?

He stood in the hot sun as Saul reiterated what Harlan had told him. He had picked a hell of a time to thrust himself back into Beth's life. Now, because he couldn't—wouldn't—make her a partner in this nasty affair, he might have lost her, again. This time, perhaps, forever.

"Are you listening?" Saul asked impatiently. He was wiry, with dark good looks, and clearly extremely bright. He had immediately zeroed in on the possibilities and the holes in Harlan's story.

"I'm listening."

"If what you've given me is garbage, I'll know within twenty-four hours. If not, I'm on the case. Maybe we have a hell of a story here. Maybe we have garbage. Watch your back while I check it out and do my own digging."

"Never mind me. Watch your own back. I don't want you ending up in a ditch on my account."

Saul's dark eyes flashed. "Won't be on your account, pal. This is my job. It's what I do, and I accept the consequences. Anything happens, shouldn't be on your conscience." His grin radiated his passion for his work. "Then again, you could go after them yourself."

Harlan laughed. "The ball's in your court now." He started across the park to the lot where he'd seen Beth. He couldn't ask her to understand being shut out of his life, not again.

Yet as he stood in her empty parking space, he remembered the feel of her smooth, wet skin against his in the shower, remembered her blue eyes upon him, her skeptical smile. He envisioned her at home, under her mass of quilts with her animals, and at work at her oak desk at Mill Brook Post and Beam. She was multifaceted and so completely herself. He was sure he wasn't finished with her or ever would be.

That was a problem for the future.

Meanwhile he would have to wait for Saul to do his job, and for the *gentlemen* who preferred that Saul didn't uncover what they were up to, if need be, to do theirs.

Maybe it was just as well Beth had gone.

7

BETH ARRIVED HOME in time for the Thursday-morning sunrise. It was a glorious splash of pale pinks and lavenders, rising over the hills where the Stiles family had toiled for generations. She had paced herself heading north, keeping in mind the limitations of her aging car and her wandering thoughts. She had decided to slink into town before dawn, instead of in broad daylight, when word would travel fast that Beth Stiles was back. Her dogs and cats and chickens and one duck greeted her gladly, for Char hadn't given them the attention Beth did. "I'll feed them," she'd informed her best friend. "There's no way I'll pet them."

Bone weary, Beth didn't keep track of who piled into bed with her. She felt welcomed. Making love with Harlan in his dismal shower would have to suffice her for a few years. Maybe forever. Men, she'd concluded somewhere near Harrisburg, Pennsylvania, were off her list, unless she was being "just one of the boys."

She didn't set her alarm and awoke around noon to an impatient chorus of barks, meows and cackles. Charity Winnifred Bradford Stiles was standing beside her bed with a meat cleaver in her hand.

"I saw your car," Char said. "I wasn't sure, though, it was you. I heard you left town in Julian's Rover. Should have known you'd come back in that damned Chevy. No, don't get up. Don't give me explanations. I've had my own dealings with Harlan Rockwood. That man—" she lowered her meat cleaver "—is trouble."

Beth's cocker spaniel leaped off the bed when she sat up. "I'd better get some locks for my doors," she said. "If you can walk right in, so can anyone else."

"You can feed your own animals today?"

"Uh-huh. I'm . . . I guess I'm home for good."

Char gave her a penetrating look. "Yeah. You're all right?"

"Fine."

"Harlan?"

She shrugged. "On his own."

"You want to talk, you know where to find me. I've got a twelve-thirty appointment. Adam and Julian are up at the mill. Thought you might like to know that they're not mad. You picked up enough slack for them when they were sorting out their love lives."

"To happier endings than mine," Beth pointed out. "Not that I'm sorting out *my* love life. I'm staying away from men."

Char let that one slide. "Where's the Rover?"

"Harlan still has it as far as I know."

"Uh-huh. Hard fellow to stay away from, isn't he?"

Beth grimaced. "He has been a bit of a bad penny lately. I think that's over. He'll probably hire someone to drive Julian's Rover back up to Vermont."

"Want to lay a small wager on that?"

"Char, I don't know what's happened to you since you married my brother. Honestly. You've turned into a scheming romantic. Pretty soon you'll quit your law practice and start writing romance novels. . . ."

"Nope. I quit my practice once and have no intention of doing so again. And I don't 'scheme.' I scrutinize the facts and make my judgments. The facts, Beth, tell me that you and Harlan—"

Beth threw a pillow at her. "Out! I'm miserable enough, without you telling me Harlan cares two figs about me!"

"What makes you more miserable, thinking he *does* care or thinking he doesn't?"

"Thinking about him at all. Now thanks for caring for my animals. I'm home, I'm staying, and I'm fine. I'll call you later."

Humming a romantic melody, Char headed on her way.

Beth crawled out of bed, making her rounds, taking comfort in the affection of her array of pets and the serenity of her home in the valley. She suppressed her dismay at the thought of her life stretching on into the future in an endless repetition of daily routines.

She had to drive through Millbrook Center and Old Millbrook to get to the mill. She pretended not to see the townspeople pointing at her, as if she'd returned from the moon. The Chevy had begun to roar. It needed a new muffler, and Beth feared for the radiator. At least it got her to Mill Brook Post and Beam.

With the windows rolled down, she sat in the parking lot for a few minutes and breathed in the cool, dry air, smelling of evergreens. She listened to the whine of the saws and the splash of the river over the rocks. This was familiar territory, and the tension and rawness she still felt would ease over time. She resolved to carry on as she had after her divorce.

Item one on her agenda was an explanation of her strange behavior over the past week to Julian and Adam.

They greeted her with their usual reserve, clearly restraining an impulse to demand an account of what she'd been up to. The stiffness of their jaws belied their cool "Glad to have you home, Beth." All was well at Mill Brook Post and Beam. Having helped Adam hold down the fort when Julian was off romancing his future wife, Holly, and having helped Julian when Adam was off romancing Char, Beth had had no worries that they'd manage for a few days without her. She, however, hadn't been off romancing anyone. Just chasing Harlan, and he didn't count. He'd told her as much himself.

So she told her brothers as much as she felt they deserved to know: that she was fine, that the Rover would be returned, that Harlan Rockwood was on his own.

"Not 'that snake Rockwood'?" Julian asked. "Plain old Harlan Rockwood."

She sniffed. "You can fill in your own adjectives."

"He tell you what kind of trouble he's in?" Adam asked.

"Wouldn't matter if he did. I'm out of it."

Adam pondered her response for a moment. "So what now?"

"Nothing. I'm back to work."

"You owe me one Land-Rover," Julian put in.

"I'm sorry." She didn't know what else to say.

"Forget it. Harlan always did turn you into hell on wheels. I guess he can afford to buy me a new Rover, if it comes to it, which it shouldn't. Seems to me Adam and I put you through enough this past year with our love lives, so we can stand it while you sort out yours."

Beth gave him a sharp look. "You been talking to Char?"

Julian grinned. "Just reading the handwriting on the wall, Beth. It's there for anyone to see."

She didn't bother to protest. She wasn't sure she'd have believed anything she said right now herself. The truth was, Harlan's intrusion into her life *had* stirred up her dreams of love and romance. If nothing else, she now could admit that the uneasiness she'd felt ever since she'd found out that Char had gone into a horse deal with Harlan Rockwood had to do with what

Harlan had meant to her and what she had meant to him. Their lovemaking and the skulduggery in Tennessee had finally laid to rest any nagging regrets about what might have been. Might-have-beens didn't count.

"You look real down, Beth," Julian commented later that afternoon, when she'd gone back to her desk and he caught her staring out the window at the view of the millpond.

"Nothing work won't cure." She sounded snappish, even to herself, and sighed, setting down her pencil. "I'm sorry. It's Harlan. You know he's always made me crazy. I've got to get him out of my system."

"Is that what you want?"

"It's what I need. I don't know anymore what I want."

"You want to come up to the house for dinner?"

She shook her head. "I need to be alone."

"It's safe?"

"Yeah," she said, thinking of Saul Rabinowitz and Harlan's bruised body. "I don't know enough to be of use to anybody."

"Call me if you need me."

Adam, however, wasn't so easily dissuaded. If Beth refused to stay at his and Char's house until they knew for sure she wasn't in any danger, he'd stay at her "shack."

"That's not necessary," Beth said. "Really. I'll be fine. Look, if I get spooked I'll get in my car and come stay with you. I'm used to being on my own. It won't bother me. No one came around while I was gone, right? Well, then, don't worry."

By evening, back at her house with her animals, Beth realized it was going to take more than one afternoon back at the mill to exorcise Harlan from her system.

She hoped he was all right.

Thought about him in the shower, inside her.

Remembered how she'd cried out for him.

Disgusted with herself, she turned up the cold water.

To burn off her frustration, she decided to work up a good sweat and take out her aggravation on several chunks of oak. Pulling on jeans and a sweatshirt, she went outside to the woodpile behind her home.

"Well, well. I never would have guessed I'd see a Rockwood woman chopping wood."

Beth flung around, ax in hand, heart pounding.

Jimmy Sessoms took a step back, clear of her ax. Breathing hard, she lowered its head into the dirt and leaned on the handle. "I'm not a Rockwood woman."

"I guess maybe you're not." He eyed her closely, somehow looking more astute than she remembered from his first visit last week. "You're Harlan's woman, though, aren't you?"

Her body tensed. "I'm my own woman. What can I do for you, Mr. Sessoms? I spoke to your client the other day. She said she has no further need for your services."

"That's what I suggested she tell you." Jimmy Sessoms drew a line through the sawdust with the toe of his running shoe. The jovial private eye he'd played last week had been transformed into a solemn professional with a mission. Beth could feel her heart thud with fear for Harlan. Sessoms continued. "I didn't think it wise for you to be poking around and getting yourself into trouble. Neither did Mrs. Rockwood."

"Good of you to mind my affairs for me," Beth said tightly.

"Tell me where your former husband is before he gets himself into more trouble than he can handle, if he hasn't already."

"Harlan's always gotten himself into more trouble than he can handle." She leaned heavily on the ax handle, steadying herself. *Now what? Harlan—I couldn't stand it if something happened to you when I ran.* "What makes you think it's any worse now than usual?"

"You tell me."

Something about him made her uneasy about revealing anything to him. "Look, Harlan's troubles aren't my problem. I told you. We've been divorced for nine years."

Once again, Jimmy Sessoms scrutinized her. She wondered if she'd underestimated his intelligence and tenacity. "So how come you followed him to Tennessee?"

Taken aback, Beth reeled and gripped the ax handle hard, to keep from disclosing her shock. She asked coolly, "What makes you think I did any such thing?"

"Eleanor Rockwood spotted your Chevrolet on her street." Evidently quite pleased with himself, Sessoms took a step toward Beth. "Vermont license plate and all."

"That doesn't mean I was following Harlan."

"What else would you be doing there?"

Her cheeks felt flushed, as if she were a twelve-year-old caught staring at a boy during class. She didn't like Sessoms's tone, his smugness, or his devious methods of dealing with her. She'd get rid of him, call Eleanor Rockwood, and advise her to get herself another private investigator.

"I don't care for your tone," she said in her best, snotty-Yankee voice. "I've nothing to hide. We're on the same side, aren't we?"

"That's what I thought, but now I'm not so sure. You've been playing games with me, Miss, right from the start, and I don't like it. Maybe I didn't make myself clear to you. Harlan Rockwood's *mother* hired me to find her boy. I'm not your enemy."

Beth decided a shift in subject was in order. "I understood you'd gone back to Tennessee yourself."

"I did. Took a flight up this morning when I found out you were back in town. I made a couple of calls. Did you see Harlan in Nashville?"

"If you think he's in Nashville, why aren't you looking for him there? One of your calls could have been to me, you know."

"Have to trust my instincts in this business," Jimmy Sessoms informed her. "And my instincts tell me you're skittish—for reasons beyond seeing a man you've been divorced from for the better part of a decade. You're no dummy, are you, Mrs. Rockwood? To be honest, I thought Harlan might be with you, that maybe you were hiding him."

"From what?"

"You tell me."

"Well, he's not here." Beth gestured with one hand, keeping the other on the ax. She was beginning to dislike Jimmy Sessoms. "You're free to look around."

"Thanks. I trust you, so I'll take your word he's not here." He laughed. "That surprise you, sugar? It shouldn't. We're on the same side, remember? I'll be staying at the Old Millbrook Inn tonight. Call me if you hear from him, won't you? He's got a lot of people worried."

Making no promises, Beth watched him leave. When his car—another Ford Taurus sedan, this time with New York plates—had disappeared around the bend, she headed back inside, bewildered by Jimmy Sessoms's visit. Was he a professional or a kook? Had he figured out what Harlan was up to? *Had* Eleanor Rockwood lied to Beth about her son having called her? Beth knew he hadn't gone fishing. Did his mother realize what he was up to?

What exactly did she herself really know? She had assumed that any clues Jimmy Sessoms had gathered were misleading ones. Was it arrogance that made her think she was on the right track?

She filled two large kettles with water and slammed them onto the stove. She hated being passively on the sidelines, letting things happen to her instead of taking charge of her own fate. On the other hand, if *she* were in Harlan's place, would she want him meddling, swooping in to rescue her? No. She would want him to mind his own damned business.

So she would mind hers.

She pulled the shades and dragged her galvanized washtub into the middle of the kitchen floor. After dumping in a bucket of cold water, then hot, she added an envelope of lily of the valley bath seeds. She leaned over the tub and splashed the water with her hands to create bubbles. Inelegant, but effective. She peeled off her sweaty, wood-chopping clothes and climbed in.

She heard a bump in the attic.

She ducked under the bubbles as best as she could and held her breath, listening.

He couldn't be here. He wouldn't have had time to get to Vermont. There was no reason. Someone in town would have spotted him and passed the word. She would have *felt* his presence before now, damn it!

Remembering the peephole, she stared up at the ceiling, trying to discern a green eye looking down at her.

"Harlan Rockwood, if you're up there," she said, "you'd better announce yourself right now, because I'm coming up. And if I find you, I'm—well, I'm getting my ax!"

She reached for her bathrobe and pulled it around her as she leaped out of the tub, dripping water everywhere. Was she losing her mind? Her old house was filled with squeaks and strange noises. She went into the kitchen, saw a meat cleaver and grabbed it instead.

There was no light on the attic stairs. She mounted them slowly, meat cleaver held tight, and listened for any sounds of a human presence. Her heartbeat accelerated.

Halfway up the stairs she heard flapping and ducked as a bat swooped across the open room and landed on the wall above her head. Beth threw her meat cleaver at it and missed by a yard. She stomped back downstairs, grabbed a blanket, came back up, two steps at a time, and tossed the blanket over the unsuspecting bat. She carried bat and blanket out the front door and left them there.

Breathing hard, she shut the door and leaned against it. Better a bat than Harlan. Better a bat, certainly, than the men who had beaten up Harlan. A bat was one of the familiar disadvantages of having purchased old Louie's place. When she fixed up the attic, there would be no more bats.

She stuck one hand into her tub. Her bathwater had gone cold. She got her bucket and began emptying the water into the sink. She dragged the washtub back into the pantry, mopped up the splashed water and hung up her towel. After a while she went out and retrieved her blanket.

The bat had flown away.

HARLAN LAY on the lumpy mattress of his makeshift bed in Beth's attic and stared at the beamed ceiling, the timbers sawn, no doubt, generations ago at the water-powered sawmill now run by the Stiles family. Beth had once explained to him the workings of the old up-and-down saws. She had a passion for saws, post and beam construction and forest management that he had appreciated, if not shared. At the time she hadn't acknowledged her passion, wanting out of Mill-brook, out of Mill Brook Post and Beam, out of New England altogether. It was strange that Beth was aware only of his rebellion against family tradition, not of her own.

Strange, too, that they'd both made places for themselves within family tradition. He couldn't give up his life in Tennessee and join the Stiles clan. He wouldn't be himself then.

So how could he expect Beth to give up her life in Vermont and join the Rockwood clan? Why was that self-destructive act expected of her? During their brief, tortured marriage, he had watched her try to become a Rockwood, try to live his life, and slowly, painfully, struggle to become someone else—a woman he didn't know. Ambivalent and then angry at having to become someone she didn't want to be, Beth had taken out her frustrations on Harlan. They'd begun to fight. Their marriage had fallen apart, and Beth had fled, back to the familiarity of her home and the much-needed love and approval of the Stiles clan.

Harlan closed his eyes, attempting to shut out his own contradictions, his own torn loyalties. He must have been mad to come back here. They were both tenacious, stubborn, committed to their own ways of life. What could be more different than his life in Tennessee and hers in Vermont?

He shifted slightly and heard the springs creak. Tensing, he remained utterly still. It was past midnight. He hoped Beth was asleep. Thank God for that bat! The damned thing had been diving at him for over an hour, and he'd about had his fill when Beth had heard the commotion above her. She'd dealt with it efficiently, missing him as he ducked behind an old bureau. She probably would have thrown a blanket over him and tossed him outside, too, given half a chance.

She'd never come back to collect her meat cleaver. A small favor she hadn't come after him with her ax.

"Madness," he breathed. "You should have gone back to Coffee County."

But Jimmy Sessoms . . . his mother . . . Saul . . .

Problems for tomorrow. He would get through the night and be gone in the morning.

IN HIS DREAM he had the sensation of plummeting down a black hole. He threw out his hands and legs in a futile effort to stop himself. He kept falling. He landed with a thunk and groaned, not sure of where he was, whether he was asleep or half-awake. He gasped for air in the blinding darkness and heard the pitter-patter of rain on a tin roof.

Then he felt the pressure of a foot on his back. "Don't move," Beth said.

The ax or the meat cleaver? He didn't move. Fully conscious now, he realized he'd fallen off his bed and landed on the floor in a tangle of blankets. Beth couldn't see his face. He wasn't sure it would help his cause if she could.

She tore back the blanket and almost ripped his head off in the process. Then she said, "You," in that mix of disgust and excitement that had always signaled her ambivalence toward him. She removed her foot from his back. He rolled over and saw she'd lowered the nastiest-looking poker he'd ever seen.

He sat up. "Would a bad guy have fallen out of bed, for God's sake?"

"I don't take chances."

"Did I scare you?"

"No," she said, standing back. "I figured it was you."

"Otherwise you'd have skipped the poker and brought your submachine gun?"

That elicited a faint smile from her. "No, I'd have snuck out and gone for the police. You know, I used to feel safe here, until you showed up."

"Sorry."

"Right."

"You don't believe me?"

She didn't reply. "Be downstairs in five minutes. I'll make coffee."

Only then did he notice the gray light in the eyebrow windows. He glanced at his watch: not quite six. Beth disappeared down the stairs. He heard the yapping clamor of dogs and cats as she let them out. He pulled on his pants and joined her in the kitchen.

She'd put a dented aluminum coffeepot onto the stove to perk and waved him off while she went into the pantry to change into her jogging clothes. Harlan felt like a trespasser. He sat uneasily at the table and watched the coffeepot steam and rattle.

When she emerged in her shorts and T-shirt, her legs long and strong and smooth, Harlan felt himself stirring and had to resist the impulse to go to her. She'd pulled her hair off her face, and he was struck by her angular beauty. He knew he wanted her. Knew the energy and spirit and cockiness that had attracted him fifteen years ago were still there, stronger, deeper, more defined.

He knew he loved her. His doubts and confusion were gone. He acknowledged his love for Beth and had a hard time concealing it.

He was in her house, uninvited and most likely unwanted. What he did next was up to her.

He got up and moved toward her. She held up a hand, stopping him in his tracks. He watched her hold her breath, could see the doubts and confusion clouding her face.

"Don't," she whispered. "I'm going for a run. I need to think. You're not what I expected to have to face today."

"What did you expect?" he asked.

Her eyes held his. "To have to begin getting used to going on without you."

He was silent. She darted out the door.

The coffee boiled over. Harlan turned off the heat, and burned his fingers on the pot. He nearly tripped over one cat, while another nuzzled against his pant leg. He nudged them both away and filled one of the mugs Beth had set on the counter. The coffee tasted burned and was strong enough to have paved Maple Street. Harlan took it onto the porch.

The rain had stopped. A dense fog blocked the view of the mountains and enclosed the house in the private world of the valley. The air smelled of damp grass and soil. Leaning against a porch post, he imagined Beth jogging in the fog, taking long strides.

He left his mug on the arm of a chair and started down the driveway, toward Maple Street. The dirt road was slick with rain. He crunched his bare toes in the mud and stretched his arms overhead, easing the stiffness from them. He inhaled the damp, cool morning air. He wasn't following her. He had no idea which way she'd gone. He was just walking, just working himself into the day. If only, for a few minutes, he could stop thinking, stop feeling.

She came up on him from behind.

He whipped around, startled, and saw her tentative smile. She didn't speak. Her route must have taken her down Maple Street first, then back up, so that he'd somehow ended up ahead of her. She wiped a red bandanna across her face and down her neck, then stuffed it into the waistband of her shorts.

"Do your feet hurt?" she asked.

"No." His voice was hoarse.

"Do you remember?" She paused, then brushed one finger down his bare arm, not looking at him. "Do you remember when we made love in the field? The horses were just yards away and could have trampled us, for all we knew, and the risk added to our excitement. We were foolish, weren't we?"

There were fields all around them. No horses, though. He said cautiously, "No, in love."

"Whatever *that* means."

"Beth . . ."

She moved closer to him, trailing her fingertips all the way down his arm to his wrist, then slid them onto his waist. She brought her arm around him and eased herself even closer, until he could feel the softness of her breasts against his chest.

Her mouth was open when it reached his. Whatever restraint he might have had left vanished with the taste of her, salty and warm. She started to sink against him, and he caught her about the hips, heard her moan as they deepened their kiss.

He didn't know if she propelled him under the maple, or if he did her. He was hardly aware of leaving the road. They fell together into the soft, green, knee-high bed of grass beneath the arching branches of an ancient maple.

"We weren't foolish." He pulled her onto himself. "We *are* foolish. Anyone due out on this road?"

"Not at this time of morning. No one can see us over the stone wall." She grinned, pulling off her shirt. "It's my land, anyhow."

"I don't want to be the subject of small-town gossip."

"You already are."

She peeled off her bra, casting it aside. It caught on a fern. Harlan smoothed his palms over her breasts and felt a familiar ache spread through him. He couldn't believe how much he wanted her.

Within minutes they'd both torn off all their clothes, tossing them into the dead leaves along the stone wall, into the grass and ferns. The rain started again. They paid no attention. Coming together in the cool, wet grass, enveloped by the fog, was an experience nothing like Harlan had known before.

"Are we too old for this?" Beth asked, her mouth close to his.

Harlan pulled her deeper into him. "Never."

She made a face. "I mean in the rain—out here."

"A dry bed would be nice, one of these days. We've got time."

Her expression darkened. "Do we?"

Before he could answer, her mouth came down onto his and they lost themselves in a new wave of passion, as the rain pelted them. Harlan gasped for air, for release. He would drown out here, making love in the rain.

Then there was quiet, the lull after the storm, and he realized it wasn't raining as hard as he'd thought.

Beth pulled on her drenched clothes. "I need to finish my run."

He reached for his own clothes and struggled to find the right words, the ones that could express his flood of emotions and ease the ambivalence he knew Beth was feeling. Before he could speak, she was dressed and had disappeared into the fog.

Alone in the rain, Harlan shook bits of grass and fern from his clothes and pulled on the sopping mess as best he could. If he got back to Beth's house and she had pulled the shades and barricaded the doors, he wouldn't blame her. When they were apart, it seemed perfectly reasonable to him to expect they could act like two rational, intelligent adults who had put their failed marriage behind them and gone on with their lives. When they were together, that seemed a totally unreasonable expectation. They had such a volatile relationship. Even on the best days of their marriage, it had been volatile, yet invigorating. He couldn't expect that volatility between them—whether invigorating or just damned frustrating—to dissipate.

Climbing over the stone wall, he reminded himself of his decision last night to get out of Millbrook this morning. First he would explain to Beth why he'd come, then she could decide for herself what to do.

He swore and peeled a briar from his pant leg. Strange how he hadn't noticed it before. The Beth Stiles influence. He headed back toward her house with extreme caution.

8

AFTER SHE'D SHOWERED, dressed and made a fresh pot of coffee, Beth felt more in control of herself. She gave up trying to pretend that she and Harlan hadn't made love and put the whole problem out of her mind. She took her coffee onto the porch and sat in one of Louie's old chairs. A tabby cat crawled into her lap. She scratched his head and listened to his purr. The rain had stopped and the fog was lifting. Streaks of sunlight penetrated the clouds and sparkled in the puddles.

She spotted Harlan coming around the bend, heading up her driveway.

"Dressed in your V.P. clothes, I see," he said easily, taking the porch steps in a single bound.

Her vice president's clothes weren't all that different from her casual wear. She dressed in serviceable shirts and slacks that would be appropriate for anything from sales meetings to running one of the saws, in a pinch. Today's outfit was stone-colored slim jeans and a coral short-sleeved cotton sweater.

"There's fresh coffee," she told him.

He was drenched and chilled. When he looked at her, her eyelashes were blacker than ever, her irises even bluer than in his dreams. "Beth, about—"

She cut him off. "Don't. Please. I can't talk, not now."

"In a hurry?"

She shook her head. "I need to sort things out on my own first."

"I understand. I'll change clothes," he said. "Be out in a few minutes. If you happen to see anyone coming, yell. It's probably best no one knows I'm here."

"Harlan . . ."

Pulling open the screen door, he grinned at her. "Wouldn't want to become a subject of Millbrook town gossip."

"You already are."

Given her house's location on a knoll in the rolling valley, she could see cars coming. Beth's curiosity was stirring again. How had Harlan's meeting with Saul Rabinowitz gone? She was annoyed at how little she knew, and because Harlan was back in her attic, shattering her stable life, arousing her passion and curiosity and telling her nothing.

She was falling in love with him all over again, crashing down that slippery, treacherous slope that could only lead to heartbreak. Harlan Rockwood wasn't what she needed in her life right now.

He returned with a mug of coffee and sat sideways on the top porch step, as he had in Coffee County, appearing relaxed and calm. He'd put on jeans and a black pullover and looked so rugged and sexy that Beth felt hot. *Resist. Stick to business. You are not going to fall in love with this man.*

The tabby jumped off her lap and climbed into his. Typical! Everyone was charmed by Harlan Rockwood.

"If you plan to stay," she said, "you're going to have to tell me everything. Not bits and pieces. Not what you want to tell me. Everything. Even then I might insist you leave."

He leveled his green eyes intently upon her. After a second he nodded. "That's only fair. I shouldn't have come," he said. "I guess I can see that now. Beth, this isn't some kind of revenge. I never had any intention of driving you crazy."

"That's what you think? That I've gone nuts?"

"Angry crazy, not insane crazy. I've thrown your life all out of balance, and I'm sorry. Mine's been out of kilter since Char came to Nashville and I started thinking about you again. I can see—well, I can see it hasn't been the same for you."

But it had—only she thought it best not to tell him so right now.

He stretched out his long legs, crossing his ankles. The cat stretched out and fell soundly asleep, as if there were no place more secure or comfortable than Harlan Rockwood's lap. "As they say, the road to hell's paved with good intentions. You got out of Nashville all right?"

She nodded. "No problem."

"I thought you'd stick around until after I'd met with Saul Rabinowitz."

"I thought so, too. I changed my mind. It seemed... I don't know, it seemed to me you were doing fine on your own and I really was meddling— however justified my meddling might have been."

He digested her words for a moment, then continued. "My meeting with Saul went well. He's on the story."

"Are you worried about him?"

"He's a pro. So are the people he's investigating. They won't want to tackle a member of the media if they can help it."

"Meaning they'd rather get to his source."

Harlan shrugged. "They already tried that and failed. I doubt they'll try again. Anyway, they're a nasty lot. For the most part, I don't think they'd go beyond cracking skulls and breaking ribs."

Beth leaned forward. "For the most part?"

"There's one individual I'm more worried about. Even him—I don't know."

"Do you know his name?"

"I'm not sure. It doesn't matter. Saul and I agreed that I'd lie low while he did his thing. I decided one of the best places I could do that was right here, even with what's happened this past week. Given your apparent hostility toward me, even if those gentlemen knew I'd been here, they'd hardly expect I'd come back for another dose of Stiles medicine for ex-husbands."

He had a point. Beth asked, "What about all your talk of not involving me in your troubles?"

"I'm not involving you. I'm just staying with you for a bit."

"Sounds like a rationalization to me."

"Saul's the one on the hot seat now. If these guys try to stop the story by giving me another pounding, they'll only confirm for Saul that what I gave him is on the money. Coming after me would be counter-productive."

"Not if they got to you and Saul both."

Harlan smiled faintly. "Then they'd have the entire *Manhattan Chronicle* and one Elizabeth Stiles on their case, in addition to the police. Charges of horse swindling would pale next to assault or even murder. No, I believe these guys are lying low as well, contemplating ways to deny the charges against them. Their plan of intimidation didn't work. Now common sense should tell them to drop it and find a new one."

The dogs climbed halfway onto the porch before they shook themselves off, sending a spray of muddy water all over Harlan. He cursed, springing to his feet and dumping the tabby.

"They're unmannerly, I know." Beth laughed.

"You're laughing."

"Well, it is funny...."

"How'll you explain a load of laundry hanging in your yard?"

"You don't think I have a washer and dryer, do you?"

"I suppose you wash your clothes in the stream."

"Nope. Wouldn't be good for the environment. I take my laundry up to Julian or Adam's and do it there. Given your behavior the past week, I wouldn't recommend the same to you. My brothers think you've gone off the deep end."

Harlan brushed himself off as best as he could. "No doubt they're not far wrong. You're going to tell them I'm here?"

"Not necessarily. I can assume you figure you aren't putting me in any danger by being here?"

"You can assume."

"What about yourself?"

"I'm trying to keep myself out of harm's way, for the time being."

"You could be wrong," Beth said.

"I could be." His drawl was liquid, sexy, utterly confident.

It would be so easy to turn her body and soul over to him for safekeeping. She'd done that once with disastrous results for them both. "Why didn't you go back to Coffee County?"

"Too obvious under the circumstances."

Beth waited for him to continue. When he didn't, she knew for sure she wasn't getting the whole truth from him. Maybe not even half the truth. Maybe he'd spun her in so many circles that even he had lost track of what was true and what wasn't.

"I suppose," she said carefully.

"So what's your verdict?"

She threw the last of her coffee over the rail into the grass. Instinct warned her to throw him out, too. Even if he was telling her the truth—and he wasn't—their lovemaking in the rain should have been proof enough that the man had a deleterious effect upon her life.

Where would he go if she threw him out?

Why had he come to Millbrook? Tossing him into the street wouldn't give her the information she wanted.

He *had* involved her in his troubles.

"Jimmy Sessoms is back in town," she said, her back to Harlan.

"Is he?" Harlan's tone was noncommittal.

"I thought your mother had pulled him off the case."

"Maybe she has. I wouldn't know."

"Then why isn't he off it?"

"Probably hasn't touched base with Mother."

Beth supposed it was possible. "Do you want to talk to him?"

"Sessoms? No."

"But if your mother . . ."

"She hired Jimmy Sessoms. She can deal with him."

"She doesn't know you're here?"

"No."

"What about Saul?"

"No."

"What if he needs to reach you?"

"I check in with him periodically."

She swung around, hard and fast, and found herself smack up against Harlan's chest. He was so damned strong these days. More muscular, harder. The feel of his arms around her . . . well, she couldn't think about that right now.

"What's your answer?" he asked softly.

She looked into his face, into the green eyes that used to drive her mad with wanting him. "I'm here, if you need me. Of course you can stay. Not upstairs, though. It's too obvious, should anyone come looking for you."

"No one will."

"Jimmy Sessoms did yesterday."

"He's different."

"I think it's safer if you camp out in the woodshed."

"With the chickens?"

"Well, no, not exactly. They have the run of the yard and seldom go inside during summer. I'm building them a coop for winter."

"Don't chickens peck out eyeballs?"

"I don't think they'd touch your eyeballs." She gave him a steady look. "You can always bar the door. Should be enough air, so you won't suffocate."

"Comforting."

She refused to budge. "Those are my terms."

He put his hands upon her hips and squeezed gently, not the squeeze of a lover, but of a friend. It felt good. It made her wonder what it would be like if she and Harlan Rockwood could actually be friends, or even lovers. Was such a thing possible? "I accept," he said, "on one condition."

"What's that?"

"The next time we make love, it's in a dry place."

She laughed, knowing there would be a next time. "Granted."

"I'm not finished."

"You said one condition."

"There's a part two. No animals. I'm not going to make love to you, worrying about chickens pecking my eyeballs out and dogs shaking their muddy selves off on me—and cats. I won't even mention what *they* can do."

"A dry place, no animals." Unexpectedly she felt giddy and acutely aware of him. "I don't know, Harlan. We might not get another chance if I have to meet those two criteria."

"Where there's a will," he said, his mouth millimeters from hers, "there's a way."

His lips touched hers ever so lightly, then again, and she murmured, "I accept your conditions."

"The hell—I'd make love to you right now in a thunderstorm, with every damned one of your animals looking on." He pulled himself away, snatching up his coffee mug from the porch floor. "You've got to get to work. I'll move my things into the woodshed."

"Harlan . . ."

He was clearly aroused. "Go on about your business and pretend I'm not here."

Deciding it was pointless to argue now, she nodded. "All right."

But later—tonight—she'd make certain that he knew damned well she understood he was holding back on her. Next time she'd insist he talk. She'd have the whole day to plan her strategy and get her hunger for him under control.

She'd had nine years to stop yearning for the rich, debonair, impossible Tennesseean she'd loved. What made her think she could accomplish in one day what she'd failed to accomplish in close to a decade?

He went up to the attic, and she yelled goodbye and climbed into her Chevy before he had a chance to answer. Glancing around her yard, she realized he hadn't come by car. Though she'd demanded to be told everything, she'd never even asked him how he'd gotten to Millbrook this time.

Naturally he hadn't volunteered the information.

"Oh, Harlan," she muttered. "You're as deadly as ever."

I think I'm as much in love with you as ever.

It wasn't a comforting thought.

IT WAS A LONG DAY at the mill.

Absolutely nothing happened. Beth wondered if she was getting addicted to excitement—the Harlan Rockwood influence. Mill Brook Post and Beam carried on its business as usual. Adam and Julian didn't bring up the subject of her jaunt to Tennessee, and neither did she. Not that she didn't think about her ex-husband. She did.

Strangely enough, she found herself perfectly capable of concentrating on her work. Whatever her feelings for Harlan Rockwood—and she couldn't have defined them herself—she no longer permitted them to incapacitate her. She would continue to function. She wasn't going to turn into a pile of mush for anyone.

Only on her way home that afternoon did she indulge a fleeting moment of panic. Suppose he'd packed up and gone into hiding someplace else? She'd sent him off to the woodshed, for heaven's sake. He could have easily decided that wasn't for him and packed off to an out-of-the-way motel with room service and hot running water.

If he *did* stick around, it had to be because of her. There was no getting around it. There were better hiding places than her ramshackle house in Millbrook, Vermont.

Having him stick around because of her brought its own measure of panic.

What would happen if one of the men on his trail caught up with him? If Jimmy Sessoms had thought to look for Harlan in Vermont, so could they.

What about Sessoms? What if he'd come poking around again and discovered Harlan sacked out in the woodshed? What if he reported back to Eleanor Rockwood? Presumably Harlan had lied to her for her own safety.

Beth sighed. Life with Harlan Rockwood would never be dull. He had said much the same about her on many occasions.

The rain had long stopped, and the last of the clouds had cleared out. The afternoon, with its cloudless, blue sky and warm, dry air, had become an ideal, late-summer day. Her windows rolled down, Beth drove slowly along Maple Street, avoiding the pits and ruts. Her car was in desperate need of a tune-up. One good bounce could dislodge the entire exhaust system, or even the engine, for all she knew. She planned to spend Saturday underneath it, having a good look.

Who knew what she'd do with Harlan around?

Her heart thudded when she turned into her driveway and parked alongside the Ford Taurus sedan with New York plates.

New York. She gripped the steering wheel, debating whether to back out of her driveway, while she had the chance, and get to town, to the police.

Then she spotted Jimmy Sessoms on her porch, his legs propped on the railing.

She shut off the engine and climbed out, not sure whether she should be relieved or not.

Sessoms waved to her. "Afternoon, Mrs. Rockwood."

She didn't wave back and remembered that he'd flown up from Tennessee, presumably arriving in Albany and renting a car there to drive up to Millbrook.

Dogs, cats and chickens ambled out to greet her. She absently patted heads and let her legs be brushed by furry bodies as she squinted in the bright sun.

She joined Sessoms on the porch. He was sipping a glass of iced tea. A tabby cat snoozed in his lap. His grin was disarming. "Helped myself. Hope you don't mind."

Beth vowed to visit the lock-and-key section of Hank's Hardware Store as soon as she got a free minute. Had Jimmy Sessoms restricted himself to an inspection of her kitchen? Or, once inside, had he snooped around for any signs of Harlan? Harlan hadn't vacated yet, but had promised he'd clean up the breakfast dishes before he did. It wouldn't take anyone, never mind an experienced private detective, very long to notice pairs of dishes in the sink of any unattached woman, such as herself. Why was she worried about Jimmy Sessoms discovering Harlan's presence? *The man is on our side*, she told herself yet again.

It was a matter of taking simple precautions. The fewer the people who knew Harlan was in town, the less chance that word would get out to the wrong individuals.

"Do you always go into people's houses when no one's at home?" she asked.

Sessoms's cheerful expression didn't waver. "Guess I'm forward by nature. Have a hard day at work, ma'am?"

"Mr. Sessoms, I'm not annoyed because I'm cranky. I'm annoyed because I have a right to be. You keep invading my privacy after I've made it as clear as I can that Harlan's business is no business of mine. Neither is whatever trouble he's in. So, if you don't mind, I have things I need to do."

Jimmy Sessoms dropped his sneaker-covered feet to the porch floor and dumped the cat off his lap. "I think you're lying. Not much I can do about it, though, is there?"

Beth adopted her iciest, most businesslike demeanor. "Goodbye, Mr. Sessoms."

His eyes were much colder than the rest of his expression. "You should talk to me, you know, before Harlan gets himself into the kind of trouble he can't get himself out of."

"That's not my problem. If it's yours, I trust you're being well paid for your efforts. Now, please go look under another rock for Harlan Rockwood. He's certainly not here."

She started inside, her back to him, assuming he would take what was much more than a hint and leave quietly.

"You change your mind," he said in his middle-Tennessee drawl. "You know where to find me. I'm not leaving town just yet. I'm a professional, Mrs. Rockwood. I can help your husband before he gets in over his head."

She turned, holding the screen door open. "Should he turn up here, I'll pass along your message. That's the best I can do. If I were you, Mr. Sessoms, I'd take my search elsewhere. If you decide to bother me again, don't be surprised if I call the police and report you for harassment."

She felt his gaze steady on her. "Just doing my job."

"Do it elsewhere."

Beth went inside, shutting the door hard behind her, careful not to slam it. She wanted to appear emphatic, not out of control. She heard Jimmy Sessoms on the creaking steps of her porch and his amiable whistling of a country and western tune and at last, the sounds of his rented car.

Only then did she get herself an orange soda and flop onto her couch in relief. She hated lying. She hated strange men creeping around her house.

Had he bugged the place?

"Lord, you are getting paranoid."

Life with Harlan was often unsettling.

"You upstairs?" she called loudly.

No answer.

She finished her drink. She would not go anxiously searching for Harlan. First she would rest for a minute and get her bearings. Jimmy Sessoms would have turned up in Millbrook whether Harlan had come back or not. Finding Sessoms on her front porch had been entirely Harlan's fault. She wouldn't have had to lie if she hadn't made love to Harlan in the field that very morning. Lying always made her hot and flustered.

Beth went onto the porch. The animals had settled down. Dogs and chickens had found spots in the shade, two cats were curled up on Louie's rickety porch chairs, the rest were off prowling. She supposed she'd have to take in the welcome mat soon; she couldn't manage many more strays without feeling overrun—especially human ones.

It might have been a perfect, hot, breezy, summer afternoon but for her churning stomach, Harlan Rockwood and his troubles. She could have sat peacefully on the porch and read a book, then listened to the Red Sox game on the radio, enjoying her solitude after a day's work.

Now she was stuck thinking about Harlan and trying to figure out a way to stop herself from falling into his arms again.

She had to preserve the fulfilling, stable life she had fashioned for herself since coming back to Millbrook. She didn't want it to change. She liked it the way it was.

Her gaze drifted to the woodshed. It looked decrepit, even more so than the house. She'd patched the leaking roof and then made shelves, hung hooks and otherwise fashioned proper spaces to store her tools and equipment. There were those in town who still didn't understand why she hadn't put in hot water first. They were people who'd never lived on their own. First you took care of your tools. Personal comfort wasn't number one on her priority list.

All in all, she could have foisted a worse place upon Harlan—Louie's crumbling barn, for instance. At least the shed was dry and in no danger of falling in on his head. Still, it was dank and windowless, and Harlan Rockwood was accustomed to finer living. He might have taken one look at his new quarters and lit out for a nice country inn.

Lit out, how? He had no car as far as she knew, not nearby, at least. He'd have had to go on foot.

Jumping lightly off the porch, she headed up the grass path to the woodshed.

The shed door was made of rough-hewn boards, and had a wooden latch near the top on the outside. The latch was secure. Even Harlan couldn't have managed that from the inside.

Evidently he had rejected his accommodations and had gone on his way—before he could asphyxiate himself within their confines—before they could end up making love there and collapse. Even as she told herself it was for the best, her heart sank. She checked inside, anyway. Every tool and piece of equipment she'd accumulated over the years was in its proper place. The chickens' half of the shed was unoccupied and only smelled of fresh hay.

She started back to the house, determined to make herself a wonderful supper and to have the kind of evening that would make her relish being alone. She had brothers, nieces, a nephew, cousins, parents, aunts, uncles, friends. Living alone didn't mean you were lonely. Life could still be wonderful. She *knew* that.

So why did she feel so damned miserable?

You have chores to do. You know from experience that life does go on without Harlan.

She pulled open the screen door and jumped back with a start. She heard Harlan singing an old tune from *The Band* and saw him cranking pepper into a steaming frying pan.

He looked up at her and grinned, and his eyes were as mesmerizing as the day she'd practically run over him at the Vanderbilt library. She'd been hell-bent on getting somewhere, and he'd been ambling along, as he always did, taking life and its ups and downs in stride. Apparently, at least. Harlan had never been as easygoing and un-Rockwood as he'd seemed.

"I feel like Old Mother Hubbard," he said amiably, "but I've managed to pull together enough fixings for a pretty decent chili. You like your food hot enough to melt your eyeballs, as I recall."

She'd stopped in the doorway. "Where'd you come from?"

"Back door." He pointed.

"You were in the woodshed?"

"God forbid. Not to be an ungrateful guest, darlin', but I checked out the accommodations and found them woefully lacking in the basic comforts—i.e. air."

"Then . . ."

"I pitched your tent."

"I don't have a tent."

"Well, then, that explains its condition. Must be something Louie left behind—looks like a relic from World War II. I found it in the attic."

Beth wished she didn't feel so much like giggling. Honestly. Why couldn't she just be neutral about finding Harlan cooking in her kitchen? "Where are you camped?" she asked.

"At the edge of the woods, over the ridge out back. There's an old hunter's lookout in a tree. I spent the better part of the afternoon up there, reading and thinking. Nice view."

"You saw Jimmy Sessoms?"

"I saw him."

"I didn't tell him you were staying here, although I can't pinpoint why I didn't. It's not as if he's an enemy, even if he has become a bit of a nuisance."

"Best to keep my presence between us," Harlan said, echoing her own sentiments.

"You did tell your mother you'd gone fishing?"

"Yes. I hate lying, but I didn't want her to worry—or to involve her."

Beth nodded, and the thought occurred to her that he'd preferred to involve his ex-wife. Somehow that was how it should have been. "Then why hasn't she called off Sessoms?"

"Probably miscommunication. From what I can gather, he seems a bit of a loose cannon. How does he strike you?"

Harlan seemed genuinely interested in her assessment. She told him, "Nosy, sexist, presumptuous—he probably treats your mother like a ninny and doesn't check in with her. I don't think it's my place to interfere."

"Wise choice." Harlan stirred his concoction, the steam making his face glow. "If I call Mother, it's likely to tip her off, and ultimately Sessoms, as to where I am. Right now, the fewer people who know, the better. We'll have to tolerate his interference for now."

"That reminds me." Beth sat down at her little kitchen table and noted that her wealthy, sophisticated, southern ex-husband looked perfectly at home. "How did you get here?"

"Oh. I drove the Rover."

"But where is it?"

"Parked in the woods, up past my tent. Four-wheel drive, you know."

"I see."

He gave her a sharp look. "Julian will get it back, Beth. I'm not trying to take advantage—"

"I know. I'm not worried about that. It's just . . . Well, Harlan, I know damned well you haven't told me everything." She put up a hand, stopping his protest before he'd uttered a word. "Now don't get defensive or start thinking up a fresh set of lies to tell me, because I don't want to hear it. When you want to 'fess up, you will. Until then we'll call a truce. I wanted you to know I know."

He had the gall not to look sheepish or even to attempt to deny a thing. "Okay."

"Then you're admitting you haven't told me everything?" she asked, more sharply than she would have liked.

"I'm not arguing with you."

"That's pretty vague."

"I suppose it is," he said, leaving it at that, and proceeded to serve the chili.

9

THE CHILI was hot and spicy and went well with their conversation. Beth and Harlan found themselves talking. Really talking. Not about pesky Nashville private detectives or tough New York investigative reporters or even faded bruises, but about their lives. About stables and horses and stray animals, and copper plumbing versus plastic, and gardening and work. About the Rockwood family and the Stiles family. About the economy and recycling and base-ball.

Over dinner and then over beer on the porch, they filled each other in on the nine years they had spent apart. Beth told him how she'd first fled home after their divorce, hadn't stayed, and had wandered about for a couple of years. She'd worked in Boston, Albany and Washington, returning to Millbrook for holidays, the occasional weekend and then for good.

"The quality-housing-kit end of Mill Brook Post and Beam was taking off," she explained, sitting on the top porch step opposite Harlan, her feet touching his. "My parents had retired, and Adam and Julian lacked any real expertise in marketing and advertising, so I jumped in. I loved it, Harlan. I still do. My brothers and I make a great team. I love being a part of a tradition that goes back well over a century, and I love the product we're selling, and how we really care about doing right by our customers, our employees and the environment. I couldn't go back to working for someone else."

"Have you ever considered not working?" Harlan asked, his eyes on her, as green and as endlessly fascinating as the foothills. Periodically he glanced out at the road.

She shook her head. "I'd go nuts."

"I suppose you would."

"I'm very aware that I'm a woman in a male-dominated field," she went on. "Most people expected me to marry and move away, or at best do bookkeeping part-time. It hasn't been easy, but my brothers and I have carved out an equal relationship—and I don't mind saying that I do feel a certain responsibility for being a role model."

Harlan downed the last of his beer. "Adam would have chucked in the towel if Char had wanted to stay in Tennessee."

"No, he wouldn't have. He might have offered, but Char never would have accepted. She knows what the mill means to him, more than it does to either Julian or to me. That doesn't make it more his, it's the way it is. If Char hadn't realized she's as much a part of this town as he is, they'd have worked out some way of being together that didn't involve sacrificing who they were."

Harlan leaned back, his knees close to his chest. The sun was dipping beyond the hills, the temperature still warm and the air refreshingly dry. "The mill's not just a job for you, it's a way of life."

"It sounds selfish...."

"No, it doesn't. It sounds honest. It's easy not to be honest, when you're just out of your teens and have your life before you. Much more difficult, when there's less time to keep fooling yourself."

Beth finished off her beer. "I'm not married to the mill. It's where I want to be. Things change. I know that. Adam's as single-minded as ever, but even he's pulled back some, now that he's put Mel's death behind him and married Char. Julian's branching out, doing his own thing. It wouldn't be so awful if I changed my routine, too, redefined my commitment. I don't want people to—well, I guess this sounds crazy, but if I do move on, I want people to realize it's because of me—not because I'm a woman, and because women do the accommodating."

"I see your point," he said thoughtfully, and she believed he did. "It's playing against a different set of expectations, but one no less limiting than being the oldest son who's compelled to conform to family tradition."

"Or the only son," she said, gazing at him with a frankness and ease she hadn't felt in years.

He smiled. "The truth is, we wanted to make our own choices about what we did with our lives, not have them determined for us by an accident of birth."

"True. But in a way I wonder if we haven't toed the family line, after all. You as a Rockwood, me as a Stiles—woman or not."

"If we have, it's because it's what we want, but you have your house down here in the valley, I have my horses. The Rockwood clan approves, but it wouldn't matter if they didn't. My stables have been my doing."

Her house definitely had been her own doing. "What you're saying is, we're stubborn."

He laughed. "I guess we are."

"Tell me, Harlan, what would the Rockwoods say if they knew you were skulking about the countryside, snitching to the *Manhattan Chronicle?*"

Grinning broadly, he suddenly looked so rakish and unrepentant—so much like the rebel she'd fallen in love with so long ago—that Beth lost her breath. He said, "They wouldn't be pleased, I can tell you. Since when do you give a damn what anyone thinks?"

She was taken aback. "I've always cared about what other people think—you have to be in a civilized society. It's a question of degree. I never cared what your family thought of my car or my decision to keep the Stiles name. Elizabeth Rockwood sounded too much like Eleanor Rockwood."

"Not that that had anything to do with your reasoning. No one would ever have confused the two of you, which is to take nothing from either of you. You're both remarkable women, in your own peculiar ways. And Mother's changed in the past ten years, too. I don't think it'd matter so much to her now what you called yourself. She'll always be Mrs. Taylor Rockwood, regardless of what we do."

"That's her choice. What about you?"

He stretched out one leg, along her thigh and bottom. "Oh, I'll always be a Rockwood."

He was teasing, and Beth nudged him with her toe. "I'm not talking about your name. Did it ever matter to you that I didn't change my name to Rockwood? You said it didn't at the time, but I've always wondered."

"It didn't matter to me what you called yourself, it doesn't and it never would. What's nice for you, darlin', is that you have a choice whether to be a Stiles or not."

"I never looked at it that way. As attached to the Stiles name as I am, I realize it's just a name. So's Rockwood. Not changing my name didn't stop me from feeling I was losing my identity in your family. Maybe having changed it would have hastened the process. I doubt it. I did love you, you know. The name business had nothing whatever to do with you."

"I know that. So did my mother, in her own way. She took it more as a personal criticism, because she's so bound by social traditions."

"I wasn't criticizing her!"

"Of course not. At any rate, the name business she could have gotten around by telling her friends you were a professional woman and young and independent. But your car, Beth, darlin', that, you have to admit, was a direct, deliberate assault on Rockwood sensibilities."

She shook her head, adamant even as she spotted the devilish twinkle in his eyes. "No way. If it had been, I'd have gotten rid of the Chevy after our divorce. You'll notice I still have it. It's just a car, Harlan."

"I know that. Do you?"

"Of course."

"So why not have gotten rid of it when it offended my parents?"

Beth sighed. "Your father, too?"

"He made several choice remarks to me about it, as I recall. He wasn't as open in his view as my mother was."

"Well, maybe I was a *little* pigheaded," she allowed.

Harlan laughed. "Maybe I egged you on because I got such a kick out of my beautiful, stubborn Yankee wife roaring through my family's well-to-do neighborhood in a 1965 Chevrolet Bel Air with no back seat. I suppose neither of us has much patience with hypocrisy and appearances."

"We could have been less judgmental."

"We could have, but we were young. If I had to take a guess, we thought people were more worked up about our little rebellions than they really were."

"Does this mean we'd still be married, if only I'd changed my name and bought a new car?"

"No. We'd still be married, only if we'd loved each other enough."

He sounded wistful, and Beth hoped he wasn't, because she had loved him. Too much. She had hung on to her car and her name, not out of spite or as a misguided act of rebellion, but out of the sense that if she didn't, there'd be nothing left of her. That didn't mean she would change her name now or give up her car. It meant that she wouldn't worry about losing herself.

"Could you have become a Stiles?" she asked quietly.

Harlan smiled and said in his most liquid drawl, "I wouldn't cut it as a Yankee mountainman."

"Only as a southern, aristocratic rakehell—"

His face clouded, and he jumped to his feet. "We've got company."

Beth stood up. "Duck inside. I'll see who it is." She recognized the Jeep coming up the road. "Relax—it's Char."

"I'm off to my tent. You'll take care of her?"

"Harlan, if there's anyone you should trust, it's Char. She's as closemouthed as they come."

He seemed unconvinced. "Not a word about me, all right?"

"Oh, all right."

He disappeared through the screen door, and Beth heard him warning off animals as he slipped out the back.

She resettled herself on the step. "Hey, there," she called to Char when she'd parked her Jeep next to the Chevy. "What's up?"

"You tell me," Char said in her lawyer's voice.

Beth knew it was going to be one of those visits. She and Char were best friends, had been since kindergarten, but that didn't mean they always got along.

Looking innocent wasn't Beth's long suit. She tried, nonetheless. "Have a seat. Can I get you something to drink?"

Char eyed Beth's beer bottle and the one Harlan had left behind. "Seems to me you've had enough to drink already yourself. Harlan getting to you?"

"Harlan? I have nothing to do with him."

"Yeah, right." Char shooed a cat off a chair and took a seat. She didn't look as if she'd been enjoying the beautiful summer's evening. "Where is he?"

"Who?"

"Rockwood."

"How would I know?"

Char squinted, and Beth could see her lawyer's mind debating her next move, figuring out exactly how she could get what she wanted from the witness. "Jimmy Sessoms is back in town."

"I know." Beth stretched out her legs and crossed her ankles, trying to look as comfortable as she could. "He stopped by here yesterday and again today."

"He seems to think you know where Harlan is, and are endangering him by not saying."

"No kidding? He's not a very good private investigator, then, is he?"

"I don't know. I think he has a point. He stopped by the mill to talk to Adam and Julian, then he came by my office to talk to me and tracked down Holly to talk to her. I don't like it, Beth. I don't like this man nosing around, and I don't like having you play games with me. If you know something I need to know, out with it."

Beth swallowed, not blaming Char one iota. "Jimmy Sessoms is the only one snooping around? No one else?"

"Why?"

"Just curious."

Char scoffed. "You are the worst liar, Beth Stiles."

"I'm not!"

"Spare me." The tabby tried to sidle onto her lap. Char shoved him unceremoniously back onto the floor. "Remember when Sessoms first asked Adam and Julian about Harlan? He said Harlan had been beaten up. Well, when Sessoms tracked me down this afternoon, I asked him how he knew. I mean, if Harlan's missing, how did Sessoms find out he'd been beaten up? You know what he told me?"

Beth shook her head, not wanting to admit Char had sparked her own curiosity.

"He told me he'd had word—he wouldn't go into detail—that Harlan was shaking the wrong tree this time, that the man was going after people who were bigger, meaner and richer than he is. The bit about his getting beaten up was an educated guess on his part, because if Harlan *hasn't* had the hell knocked out of him, he soon will. If these guys don't just go ahead and kill him." Char took a breath, got herself under control. "Beth, the man has a white-knight complex. He's in over his head, and so are you."

"Thanks for your concern. I'm having a quiet evening out here in the country."

"There's more." Char got to her feet and paced, the tabby at her heels. "I did some digging, and if I put this and that together, I keep coming up with the name Lord Arthur Penmountain."

"*Who?*"

"He's English—stinking rich, and the perfect stereotype of the upper-class nobleman. He's the one who bought the ringer from Harlan's crooked trainer. You know—the swindle that practically ruined me last year. I figure Harlan found out Lord Penmountain was responsible for the whole fiasco and had put the trainer up to it."

"What's this guy's reputation?"

"Pristine, which worries me. Nobody's that pure, not in the horse or any other business, if only because even well-intentioned, good people make mistakes." Char crossed her arms over her chest. "Penmountain's one hell of a windmill to go after. He's connected. If he's dirty, there's no fighting him alone, and I don't care if you are Harlan Rockwood."

"Char . . ."

She shook her head and swooped down all at once, picking up Harlan's beer bottle. "You've never drunk more than one beer at a time in your life, especially when you're alone. Tell Harlan to take care of himself, cool his heels, and if anything happens to you on his account, he'll have me and two irate mountain-men to answer to."

Beth was losing patience. "What happens to me is my responsibility, not his or anyone else's."

"Oh, Lord," Char groaned at the sky, then fastened her dark eyes on Beth. "You are in love with him again. Beth, I'm happy for you, and I know he probably loves you, too. You are out of your mind if you get involved with him now. Penmountain's one nasty and powerful opponent. Let Harlan—"

"I don't 'let' Harlan," Beth interrupted. "We are who we are. You know, if it weren't Penmountain, it'd be someone or something else. Last year it was you. The man doesn't lead a dull life."

"This isn't winning the Kentucky Derby or tracking down a crooked trainer. Sessoms may not be the most ethical P.I. I've ever known, but I think he's on target when he says Harlan's shaking the wrong tree this time. You watch yourself."

"Char, I told you—"

She shook her head again. "No, Beth, no more lies. Don't tell me the truth, if you can't. Please spare me the lies."

She sprinted down the stairs, and Beth watched her leave. She didn't like any of this—Jimmy Sessoms pestering her family and friends, Harlan Rockwood hiding out in Millbrook, this Lord Arthur Penmountain. The whole mess was getting more and more dangerous.

It rankled that Char knew more about what was going on than Beth did, even if most of her "facts" came from guesswork and her own connections in the thoroughbred-horse world.

"I can see what makes her a good lawyer," Beth muttered.

What are you? she asked herself.

A woman who'd turned to mush under Harlan's spell. Who was letting him keep her in the dark because it suited him.

She snatched up the two beer bottles and went inside. She cleaned up the dishes and looked out at the sunset. Nothing she did worked to settle her nerves. She was edgy, restless and frustrated at having to remain ignorant of the full dimensions of the mess Harlan was mired in.

There was only one thing to do—find Harlan's tent and tell him she wasn't going to play by his rules any longer. If he insisted, then off he went, out of her life for good. There was only so much she could take.

HARLAN ASSUMED that the creature charging through the woods toward his tent had to be one Elizabeth Stiles, if only because a bear would have less reason to come after him. He leaned against a gnarled apple tree, so old it could have been planted by Johnny Appleseed himself. Its arching branches groped for sun in the overgrown clearing, where he'd pitched his ancient tent. It was a wonderful spot to camp, full of low-growing wild blueberry and huckleberry bushes. Songbirds kept him company.

He sensed Beth's frustration and her unwillingness to call to him, lest someone else be skulking about her woods. Even enraged she remained rational and logical. That capacity to think *and* act was one of the many things he admired about her. She was clearly on a tear.

Whatever Char had come to tell her best friend couldn't have helped Beth to resign herself to waiting passively. He plucked a blade of straw grass and stuck the end into his mouth as Beth bounded over the stone wall. An ordinary human being might have tripped or at least taken great care on the loose rocks. She'd been climbing over stone walls all her life.

Chewing the end of his blade of straw grass, he watched her land at his toes. She brushed back a strand of hair that had whipped into her face and glared at him.

"Lord Arthur Penmountain," she said.

Hell.

She was plainly delighted with herself. "Name ring a bell?"

"Char should mind her own business before *she* lands up hiding in the woods."

"Then she's right? The man you're after is this Penmountain character?"

"I'm not after him," Harlan said. "He's after me. My only intention is to tell the truth. If that disturbs him, so be it."

Her eyes darkened in the failing light. "You want Saul Rabinowitz to write an article for *Manhattan Chronicle* that will expose Penmountain as a crook?"

"His racing operation in this country needs close examination. I merely put Saul onto the story and presented evidence I'd compiled to . . ." He searched for the right word. "To energize him."

"Does anyone else know what you're up to besides Saul?"

"Obviously Penmountain does."

"Penmountain must have found out your mother hired Sessoms and tried to learn if he'd figured out where you were. Probably tipped Sessoms off that you were in over your head."

"Hyperbole," Harlan scoffed.

"Yeah, I guess. You haven't had anyone smack you around in over a week."

He ignored her sarcasm. "Precisely."

She groaned and flopped into the grass next to him. The fire had gone out of her anger. She studied him closely, her lips drawn tight. There wasn't a smidgen of country-girl naïveté in her, especially where he was concerned.

"You could have told me about Penmountain," she said.

"I did. I just left out his name. Does it matter?"

"No," she allowed reluctantly. "I guess it doesn't— unless he gets to you and Saul, and I end up having to go after him myself."

"You would?"

"Of course."

"You don't know Saul, and we...I don't know what we are to each other."

Her expression softened. She said, "Maybe we should let that one go for now, until Saul does or doesn't do his article and the dust settles a bit. What you are, for sure, is a friend. You weren't a friend ten years ago."

"We're lovers, too," he said, his voice thick as he remembered the shower in Coffee County and the rain-soaked field that morning.

She looked uncomfortable, as if he'd reminded her of something unpleasant, yet he knew it wasn't that.

Beth Stiles had always enjoyed their lovemaking as much as he had. Sex had never been a problem in their relationship.

Not wanting to deepen her discomfort, he threw out his grass blade among the blueberry bushes. "Like my tent?"

"It is a relic, isn't it? I think World War I's closer on target than World War II. Is it comfortable?"

"Relatively. An air mattress would be nice, and it does smell a bit mildewed. I've left the flaps open, with hopes of airing it out before tonight."

She glanced at him with some amusement. "I'm a terrible hostess, aren't I?"

"Squatters have no rights."

He spoke to her back; she had dropped to her knees and started to crawl inside the disreputable pup tent.

"Smells a *bit* mildewed? It reeks!"

"You always did have a keen sense of smell," he told her, following her inside.

There was very little room for the two of them. His long legs got tangled with hers.

"Char and I used to sleep out in a pup tent," Beth said, folding her legs in front of her. "We'd tell ghost stories and plot how we were going to get out of Millbrook. Always this sense that Millbrook was our destiny and there was no escaping it. No reason to. It's hard to explain."

"You don't have to," he said. "I feel the same torn loyalties to Tennessee."

"It's where you belong."

He nodded. "Yes, but not at the expense of . . ."

His voice faded, but Beth prodded him. "Of what?"

"I don't want to lose you again, Beth."

His mouth found hers, and he remembered a fishing trip with Beth when they had made love until dawn in a tiny tent. Lumpy tufts of grass beneath them or not, he knew this night would be theirs, too.

"Stay with me," he whispered.

THEY MADE LOVE for a second time that night under the pale light of the stars and the half moon. During their first, playful lovemaking, Beth had pretended to swat a mosquito on Harlan's thigh. He had retaliated in kind. Now, as they lay on a pile of worn, soft quilts Harlan had swiped from her attic, they were silent.

Beth filled herself with the scents of the woods and of this man, the man who had become such an integral part of her life, of her being. She stroked his hard, sinewy body, concentrating on transmitting her passion and love through her fingertips, her tongue, her very skin. Words having failed them, their bodies took over, communicating not only aching need, but also trust. She curved her palm over the taut muscles of his thigh and felt him lifting his hips, then thrusting, gently, powerfully, into her.

No more pretending. No more apparitions and dreams and repression. She filled herself with the sheer, bold reality of him and gave herself to him as she never had before. No more denial.

"Yes," she whispered, "oh, yes."

Her eyes were open. Taking in everything, she saw the stars and the moon through the battered screen. Looking at Harlan's face in the light, she saw him smile, saw the emerald green of his passion-filled eyes.

"Let me love you," she murmured.

"Always."

SHE LEFT AFTER MIDNIGHT. Watching her pull on her tangled clothes, Harlan realized that she'd bounded after him through the woods in her bare feet. His wild, mad, beautiful country girl. No. She was every inch a woman.

Unwilling to spoil the mood with talk, they parted with a firm kiss and a promise of a huge breakfast and endless pots of strong, hot coffee in the morning.

Beyond the break in the stone wall that marked the end of the woods, he stumbled on a gnarled root and slowed his pace, suddenly mindful of roots and ruts and stones and stray animals. Another stumble would alert her to his presence.

Moving cautiously, he went the long way round to the front of her house. He crouched in the brush, letting it conceal him.

He had a bird's-eye view of Beth's strange little house in its beautiful setting, with its overgrown yard and all its potential. In its own way, the place was as idiosyncratic as she was. He could envision putting his own stamp upon its quintessential New Englandness. A rail fence, perhaps, a fence bursting with roses, and irises. Lots of irises. And perhaps a rebuilt barn and a horse or two.

He pushed back the dream and focused on reality.

There was a light burning in the kitchen. He presumed she had no outdoor light. Had she barricaded her doors?

The tent had been for her benefit. A ruse. He had known she'd have to check out his living quarters with some concocted excuse. With Elizabeth Stiles, one had best be prepared.

There was no way he was going to leave her alone, at the mercy of Lord Arthur Penmountain and his hired goons. Why else, Harlan thought, would he have returned to Vermont?

Settling in for the remainder of the night, he nibbled on some tiny wild blueberries. The woman probably didn't need his protection. Still, the potential threat—however small—against her was his doing and therefore his responsibility.

He thought of hot coffee, the warmth of her morning smile, the feel of her strong, smooth body, and sat very still, awaiting the dawn.

10

IT WAS A BRIGHT, gorgeous August Saturday. Beth was certain she wouldn't get to creep around under her car or make any headway with installing hot water. She awoke early and had a quick sponge bath in the kitchen, before Harlan or her brothers or Saul Rabinowitz, Jimmy Sessoms or Lord Arthur Penmountain and his thugs could burst in. She pulled on khaki shorts, a T-shirt and sneakers, and decided to skip her run. Her life-style over the past week was catching up with her.

While the coffee perked, she did her morning chores. She wasn't surprised to find Harlan parked at her kitchen table when she returned, a steaming mug in front of him. There were dark circles under his eyes, and the lines in his forehead appeared deeper this morning.

"Didn't sleep much?" she asked, pouring herself a cup of coffee.

"A little. Guess I'm getting soft in my middle years. How'd you sleep?"

She grinned. "Soundly."

He dispensed with further pleasantries. "I need to use your telephone."

Leaning back in her chair, she gestured to the big black phone on the wall next to the refrigerator. "Be my guest."

"Would you mind?"

"Mind what? Oh. You want me to leave so you can conduct your skulduggery in private?"

"Beth . . ."

"No, it's all right. I'll give you fifteen minutes."

To her relief, he didn't bother to make any excuses or try to tell her she shouldn't be irked. She was still being shut out. He had told her nothing last night, beyond what she had already learned from Char.

There was plenty to do outside in fifteen minutes. Brush a couple of dogs. Pick black-eyed Susans. Search for eggs. Chop wood. In her frustration, Beth only managed to sit on her wood-chopping stump and wonder whatever had possessed her to think she could be a full and equal partner in Harlan Rockwood's life.

She could have eavesdropped on him, but didn't. It was her own way of showing herself that even if he lacked honor and decency, she did not.

All the man had asked for was a little privacy.

When the fifteen minutes were up, she went back inside, promising herself that she wouldn't interrogate him. She wouldn't let her curiosity or her annoyance show. She was a woman of thirty-four who didn't need to be personally insulted just because her ex-husband wanted to use the phone in private.

He'd gotten out eggs, milk and oil and was whipping up a batch of pancakes at the kitchen table. Beth slid onto her chair. "Everything all right?" she asked.

"I'm meeting Saul."

Her throat tightened. "May I ask when and where?"

"I'd rather—" He broke off with a sigh and cracked an egg into a small, crockery bowl of milk. "He's coming here."

"*Here?*"

"To Millbrook. I'm meeting him at one of the abandoned buildings at the old academy. At one o'clock this afternoon." He paused, whisking in the egg. "Alone."

"He's on the story?"

Harlan's jaw was as hard-set as she'd ever seen. "Yes."

"Why does he need to see you? Can't you tell him what he needs to know over the telephone?"

"No. I have—" He broke off again. Telling another person his business went against his grain. "I have material he needs."

"Material?"

"Evidence. Against Penmountain."

"Holy—"

"Beth, I want you to go to Adam's or Julian's and stay there for the day until this is over. Someone could follow Saul."

"Then why the hell'd you tell him to come to Millbrook?"

"Because I can't leave."

"I don't get it. If you're so damned concerned about getting me involved, why?"

"I took the liberty of calling Adam and Julian. They'll be down in about an hour." He turned and smiled weakly at her, knowing he'd crawled back into the doghouse. "Time enough for us to have our huge breakfast."

All Beth could say, in her most scathing tone, was "*Men.*"

Harlan gave her a devilish grin. "Aren't we terrific?"

ADAM STEERED HIS TRUCK past Old Millbrook Common. He deftly maneuvered it along the winding road, the loss of his left hand barely bothering him these days. His old, grim-faced demeanor, so natural to him before he'd married Char, had, however, returned.

He glanced at her. "Don't sulk."

Beth waved a hand in dismissal. "I'm not sulking, I'm thinking."

"So far as I can see, calling me to come fetch you was the first thing Harlan's done this past week that makes any sense. Time you pulled your hand out of this boiling pot."

"Harlan told me pretty much the same thing when I left Nashville on Tuesday. That's what doesn't make any sense. Why would he come back to Millbrook?"

"When he wants you to know," Adam said, "he'll tell you."

If her brother were in her place, she supposed, he would be satisfied that Harlan had told her where and why he was meeting Saul Rabinowitz. Adam wasn't curious by nature and could easily accept that there were things he didn't have a right to know. Beth knew she wasn't like that, particularly not where Harlan Rockwood was concerned.

"Do you think he and this Saul Rabinowitz know what they're doing?" she asked. She had told Adam everything she knew—only to discover that he'd already learned as much on his own and from Char. That had grated.

"Guess they'd better."

"Well, that's comforting. Maybe we could go out to the academy and make sure."

"Maybe we can just mind our own business, like we promised Harlan we would."

She scowled, knowing there was no point in arguing when her brother had given his word. All the same, she couldn't resist adding, "Would you mind your own business, if it were *me* off to pass evidence of wrongdoing against a powerful man like Penmountain to a New York reporter?"

"You're family. Harlan's not." Beth saw Adam glance at her and almost smile. "Not yet, at any rate."

She groaned. "Oh, please."

Since there was no changing Adam's mind once it was made up, she gave up the attempt. Maybe he and Harlan had a point.

Nonetheless, she worried. She couldn't bear to think of anything happening to Harlan. Would they stop at superficial cuts and bruises this time? Not likely.

"Don't worry," Adam said, reading her mind. "Harlan knows better than any of us what he's up against."

"I hope so."

Having it out made her feel better. After ten long years she was once more capable of admitting that she hoped for the best for Harlan Rockwood, was capable of worrying and caring about what happened to him—and of loving him.

"YOU SURE KNOW how to pick 'em," Saul Rabinowitz said as he followed Harlan up to Beth's woodshed. "The lady lives here all alone?"

"For now."

"Must be hard as nails."

Harlan pushed the wooden latch, and the door swung open. "She is."

He saw Saul wrinkle his nose as he peered into the darkness. "After you."

"Of course."

With Saul on his heels, Harlan entered the shed, leaned over the waist-high partition and dipped his hand into the hay. He had hated lying to Beth. Yet he had done so because he had seen no other choice.

"The big guns at the *Chronicle*," Saul said, "will never believe this. The goods on Lord Penmountain hidden in chicken manure."

"Just hay. The chickens spend the summer free-roaming."

"What a life."

Harlan didn't know if Saul was referring to the chickens, to Beth or to both of them. He didn't ask. Fishing around, he came up with the large, plastic-coated envelope he had hidden there yesterday afternoon. He felt no rush of victory, not even relief. Nothing was finished, not yet. He handed the envelope to Saul.

"You have copies?" the reporter asked.

"No. You have copies. The original's in my safety deposit box in Nashville."

"Don't trust me?"

"Just a precaution."

"In case Penmountain's goons come after me?" Saul grinned, as if he relished the prospect. Harlan recognized that he was too much of a professional to court unnecessary trouble. It was one of the reasons he'd sought out this particular reporter over countless others. "I'm not sweating it. When he finds out I'm on the story, Penmountain'll call off the goons and drag in the lawyers. Mark my words."

Harlan was counting on as much himself. "I hope you're right."

"Something like this I rarely miss. Mind if we get out of here? I feel like something big and ugly's going to scream out of the woodwork after me."

Harlan laughed. "You can take on a crime syndicate, but life in the country..."

"Yeah," Saul said. "Doesn't it give you the creeps?"

"I DON'T LIKE THIS," Beth said.

Adam slowed the truck. Jimmy Sessoms's rented Ford Taurus was blocking Adam's narrow, steep driveway. "Neither do I."

Sessoms came around the front of the car and gave Adam his most cheerful, good-ol'-boy smile as he walked up to the truck window. "Nice place you got up there. Don't think I'll try that driveway, though. Wouldn't want anything to happen to my car." He stooped, looking across Adam to Beth. "'Morning, Mrs. Rockwood."

"Mr. Sessoms," she replied.

"How's Harlan this morning? Now, now. No more arguing. I know he's up at your place."

Before she could make her umpteenth denial, Adam spoke up. "If you'll move your car, Mr. Sessoms, we'll—" He stopped, and Beth heard his sharp intake of air. "Oh, hell."

She started to speak, then saw the long-barreled gun Jimmy Sessoms was leveling at her older brother's head. "You can stay here," Sessoms told Adam, "and I'll take your sister on back to her place. She and I'll talk to Harlan together."

"Why the devil won't you listen?" Adam demanded. *"Harlan isn't there."*

Gathering her wits, Beth cautiously curled her fingers around the handle of the passenger door. She had no idea what Sessoms would do next. She only knew that she wouldn't abandon her brother. Or, if it came to that, Harlan.

"Mrs. Rockwood and I," Sessoms said, "we know better, don't we, ma'am?"

Despite his charming drawl, Sessoms's eyes were hard. Then, in a swift motion, he flipped the gun around. Guessing what was coming, Adam jerked the truck back into Drive and stepped on the gas pedal, but couldn't move fast enough; the gun came down on the side of his head, hard. Beth yelled, but could see her brother was out cold. The truck slid forward, toward the ditch at the base of the driveway.

Sessoms backed off, giving Beth the few seconds she needed to push open the passenger door and leap out of the moving truck. She landed on her feet. Unable to sustain her balance on the steep side of the ditch, she fell to her knees. She couldn't run up to the house. Char might be there, and Abby, David, Emily. Three children and her best friend. There was no way she would lead a man with a gun to them.

Not that she would have had a chance.

As she stumbled to her feet, she saw Jimmy Sessoms standing on the edge of the small culvert at the base of Adam's driveway, his gun pointed at her. She had no idea how good a shot he was, and had no intention of finding out.

She swore.

"Not very ladylike," he said.

"My brother..."

"I didn't kill him. If you light out of here and make me chase you, though, I might."

She nodded and followed him to his rented car. He nudged her in and pushed her into the driver's seat. The keys were in the ignition. "You take the wheel. I'm not out to hurt anyone, but one false move and I'll shoot."

"Great." she said under her breath. "Where are we going?"

"Your place, of course."

She acquiesced, unsure whether or not she should be glad that Harlan wouldn't be there.

"WHAT'S YOUR NEXT MOVE?" Harlan asked as he walked Saul to his car, an ancient sports car that looked right at home parked next to Beth's Chevy.

"Go over this stuff—" he held up the envelope "—and attach myself to my computer until I finish writing this story. Convince my editor to give it a big play. Don't worry, Rockwood. It'll get done. Penmountain's out of business."

"You can use my name."

"Love you honorable southern types. Yeah, I will if I need to. Ever think of giving up the good life and becoming a reporter?"

Harlan smiled. "Never."

"Well, you didn't just open a can of worms with this one, pal. You opened a barrel of snakes." Saul smiled. "I smell a Pulitzer. Stay in touch, okay?"

"You, too."

They shook hands, and Harlan stayed put as Saul climbed into his battered car.

Put on the alert by the sound of an approaching car, Harlan spotted the Ford Taurus Jimmy Sessoms had rented barreling toward them.

"Move it, Saul." Harlan didn't bother darting for the woods, not this time. All his senses told him something was wrong. "We've got company. Head straight down Maple. It'll lead somewhere."

"Got it. You'll be okay here?"

"If I'm not, nail Penmountain to the wall."

"Oh, I'll do that, anyway."

He sped off in a cloud of exhaust fumes. Harlan stood steady on the dirt driveway, resisting the temptation to go for Beth's ax. An escalation of violence wasn't what he wanted. It was tough to plead innocence with an ax in your hand.

All the same, when he saw Beth, white-faced, behind the wheel, he would have gone after Jimmy Sessoms with a paring knife, and almost did with his bare hands. He checked the impulse. He would have to wait for his opening. *Make* one.

Nothing could happen to Beth.

Nothing.

He loved her more than he'd ever thought he could love anyone.

The car scrunched to a stop. Holding the gun on Beth, Sessoms dragged her with him out through the passenger door.

She looked fit to be tied. "What're you doing here?" she demanded. "I thought you were going up to the academy! Dammit, Rockwood, you *told* me . . ."

"I lied," he said.

There was no fury like that of a stubborn, gorgeous Yankee who'd been lied to one time too many. She called him enough unkind names to prove that she worked around burly mountain men sawyers, and her pale face turned red.

Jimmy Sessoms warned her to shut up.

"Shoot him," Beth said, gesturing madly toward her ex-husband. "Go on and shoot him. He *deserves* to be shot. Here I am, trying to save his miserable hide, and he has the gall to be here."

"Mrs. Rockwood, if you don't keep quiet . . ."

"Dammit, then *I'll* shoot him!"

She went for Sessoms's gun, transforming herself from a maniac into a coolheaded opponent with such speed and electricity that he was caught off guard. The gun went flying. Harlan, who'd hoped she was putting on an act when she started to talk about having him shot, snatched up the gun.

Sessoms had Beth's arm twisted around her back and, no doubt, was ready to break it or strangle her. Harlan leveled the heavy gun at him.

Red-faced and perspiring, Jimmy Sessoms hesitated. Harlan understood why. Sessoms had to know he wouldn't kill him, and breaking the arm of one exasperating Yankee might be worth a bullet in the arm or leg.

He dropped her wrist, and she darted out of his reach. Harlan bristled. "You could have gotten us both killed."

"Well, isn't *that* the pot calling the kettle black!"

"You meet Rabinowitz?" Sessoms asked.

"You were five minutes too late."

Beth fastened her most vicious gaze on Sessoms. "Good. Now you can pray my brother's all right."

Harlan felt his heart pounding, harder even than when he and Beth had been in danger. Okay, so he'd dragged her into this mess with him. They were a team. Partners, lovers. He'd given her countless opportunities to pull back. But Adam?

"Beth?"

She didn't have to answer. They both turned at the sounds of sirens and speeding vehicles. Probably for the first time in the last century or two, Maple Street was crowded with vehicles. Police cars, trucks, a brand-new Jeep Cherokee. The entire Millbrook police department—two officers—had apparently been called out. And there was Julian, looking fierce, Adam, blood dripping down the side of his head, and Char, leading the pack with her tire iron.

"People around here look after each other," Harlan observed.

Beth smiled at him. "Yeah, they do."

"TOWN'LL BE FEEDING off this one for years," Julian grumbled.

Beth sniffed. "At least you'll be around to hear the gossip."

He merely glowered at her.

"Marry her," Adam ordered Harlan, as if his sister had no say in the matter. "Millbrook can't take much more of this."

Beth started to protest that "this" had nothing whatever to do with her and Harlan's relationship, but with her ex-husband's propensity for trouble and his closemouthed ways. She was thoroughly ignored. Adam, Julian and Char—who'd provided her unrequested legal advice for free—headed to a local tavern for drinks. Beth and Harlan were pointedly not invited, she noted.

There was nothing for her to do but drive her ex-husband back to her place. "I suppose," she said, "Saul would be upset if the *Millbrook Bulletin* scooped his story."

Harlan laughed. "Upset isn't the word. I have a feeling Lord Penmountain wouldn't hold a candle to Saul on a tear."

"Saul doesn't have anything to worry about, does he? You told the police the bare essentials. It's unlikely Jimmy Sessoms is going to blab."

His laughter faded. "It's a question of priorities."

They drove along in silence. Beth turned down Maple Street and bit her lower lip hard, so she wouldn't ask. She hadn't yet and she wouldn't. If Harlan wanted to tell her what he knew about Sessoms and why he'd lied, he would.

She pulled into her driveway and welcomed the peace, the chill in the breeze, the scurrying of her animals. Only someone as in love with him as she was could know how exasperating he could be.

Harlan grinned at her over the top of the Chevy. "All those nasty names you called me. You *were* putting on an act?"

"Not a chance, Rockwood."

He was unperturbed. "You had some new ones in there."

"I was just getting warmed up."

"All bark and no bite, isn't she?" he said to her cocker spaniel, patting his head. "We know how to handle Yankee crankpots."

It was all the warning she got.

Catching her as she came around the front of the car, he scooped her up, one arm around her middle, and hauled her onto the porch. She was not a light woman. Still, he had no problem and wasn't even breathing hard when he kicked open her front door and carried her inside.

He dropped her onto the couch. His face was slightly red. That could have been from pure aggravation. He looked as if he'd done nothing more strenuous than haul in a sack of potatoes.

"Time we talked," he told her.

Sprawled on the couch, Beth tucked up her feet under her and sat sideways. "I've been talking right along. *You*'re the one who hasn't been talking."

"All right." He raked one hand through his hair. "It's time *I* talked."

"Bravo."

"Don't give me that sanctimonious look." He pointed a finger at her. "You, darlin', are no saint. Taking on Sessoms like that . . . It was enough to turn a simple crook into a killer!"

She scowled. "You're welcome."

"I'm not thanking you!"

"Are you going to keep shouting at me?" she asked calmly.

Tightening his hands into fists, he sat down on the soft, cozy couch next to her feet. "No, I'm not." He looked at her; his eyes had never been so green. "It's fear, you know."

She couldn't speak. Filled with emotion, she realized how accustomed she'd grown to doing exactly as she pleased, with nothing to concern her except the occasional grumblings of Char and her brothers. Building a life with another person required compromise, caring and courtesy. They were things she would both expect and give.

"When Sessoms dragged you out of his car at gunpoint—" Harlan broke off, briefly shutting his eyes. "Here I'd come so close—we'd come so close. For a split second, when I questioned my assessment of Sessoms, I imagined having to go on again without you. It was a bleak picture, not one of the life I wanted."

"Harlan . . ."

He held up a hand and cleared his throat, getting himself back under control. "Sessoms first. We'll get to us. There'll be time."

She nodded. She knew there would be.

"I knew he was a greedy little bastard. After my mother hired him, he caught wind of what was happening. My guess is Penmountain's men suggested it'd be more profitable if he turned me over to them instead of simply reporting my whereabouts back to my mother."

"That's how he knew you'd been beaten up. It wasn't just a lucky guess."

"Right. I'd hoped he'd buy the story about my having gone fishing, but he didn't. He kept pushing. That confirmed my suspicions. I stopped in at his office to warn him off, but he'd already headed up to Vermont. So off I went."

"Wait a minute." Beth sat up straight. "You couldn't have had time to drive the Rover up. Sessoms was here on Thursday. So were you."

"I flew and took one expensive cab from Albany."

She stared at him. "Another lie?"

"A white lie." He smiled, leaning toward her. "If I'd told you I'd flown, you'd have known I had a bee in my bonnet about something, and there'd have been no peace until you knew what. As it was, there was precious little peace."

"So where's the Rover?"

"In Tennessee. I already spoke to Julian about it."

Julian wouldn't get mad at Harlan, though. He'd scream and yell at her for borrowing it in an emergency. "My brothers always had a soft spot for you. Did they know Sessoms was from the wrong side of the river?"

He shook his head. "I didn't tell anyone, even Saul."

"Then you didn't come here to cool your heels and be with me. You came here to nail Sessoms."

"I came here, you silly ass, out of deep concern for your safety. As much as you talk about me jumping on my white horse, you, lady, have damned little room to talk. You'll jump on anything streaking past you at ninety miles an hour. You'll think first—yeah, sure. Then you'll jump anyway."

She laughed. She couldn't help herself. "We do make a pair, don't we?"

"A hell of a pair."

"Why'd you lie about meeting Saul?"

"Because I figured something would happen, and if you decided to spy on me or were forced to take Sessoms to me, you'd go to the wrong place. I had no idea you'd end up back here." He shrugged off his mistake. "Can't win 'em all."

She sighed. "I guess it worked out in the end."

He looked at her, his eyes lost in the shadows of the afternoon. "Did it?"

"We're both alive."

"We've been alive the last nine years."

"Yes. We needed those years, Harlan. We needed those years, so we can have now."

"And tomorrow?"

"And tomorrow."

"Forever," he whispered, and his mouth descended to hers.

Epilogue

THEY WERE MARRIED three weeks later, with none of the fanfare of the first time, but with all of the hope, the promise, and ten times the confidence. The ceremony took place in the front yard of old Louie's place. Beth had even mowed for the occasion, except for the section over by the woodshed where wildflowers continued to bloom. She and Harlan had picked black-eyed Susans and daisies for the buffet table, which they'd covered with handmade quilts they'd found in the attic. Glowing from the attention of the national media he'd garnered with his exposé on corruption in the thoroughbred-racing world, Saul Rabinowitz told them it was their good fortune he wasn't a gossip columnist, because he'd have had a field day with this event. As he'd predicted, Lord Penmountain had called off the thugs and brought in the lawyers. Beth was delighted. She wouldn't have to explain hired security guards to her wedding guests.

She'd forgotten about her animals, though, and a few moments before she and Harlan said, "I do," she glanced back and saw the tabby swirling around

Eleanor Rockwood's ankles. Eleanor, far more gracious than Beth, as a nineteen-year-old rebel, had been able to recognize, picked up the cat and held him, purring, until the ceremony was safely over. Then she discreetly went inside, no doubt to wash her hands. Beth didn't think to tell her about the lack of hot water.

Eleanor caught up with her daughter-in-law at the reception. "What a charming place you have up here. The view is priceless. I know you and Harlan will make it into a lovely home. It reminds me somewhat of my childhood in Coffee County, before I met Taylor. Don't you think washtub baths are romantic?"

Beth nearly choked. "Yes—yes, in a way they are. But I think they'd lose some of their romance in the dead of winter."

Not that winter needed to be a problem. She and Harlan would have two homes, his "farm" on the Cumberland River, her ramshackle house in Vermont. Each would give a little. He would downsize his stables to accommodate new interests, like gut rehabs of old New England homes. She would redefine her role at Mill Brook Post and Beam, recognizing that the roles of her brothers and herself had been ebbing and flowing since they'd first gone into business together. She would hire out the boring parts of her job, keep the interesting ones and go on from there.

Camped in the fields one night, they'd agreed that compromise was an act of strength and independence, not of weakness and dependence.

"Oh, Beth," Eleanor Rockwood was saying, "I know you didn't have a chance to meet my Aunt Tilly. You never met when you and Harlan were first married. She was away doing mission work in Africa, remember? Aunt Tilly, I'd like you to meet my daughter-in-law, Elizabeth Stiles. Beth, Tilly Duncan."

Beth was almost speechless at her mother-in-law's introduction. As she shook the tiny, elderly woman's hand, for the first time she really felt as if she belonged among the Rockwoods, simply as herself.

After the reception, Harlan couldn't wait to get away. They'd cleared their calendars for a week. No interviews, no lawyers, no horses, no dogs, no cats, no chickens, no mill. Beth's one request was that wherever they went, there should be hot running water. Harlan's one request was that they go in her Chevy. It'd be like the old days, he'd said. She didn't believe him. She thought he simply wanted to run her car into the ground.

They went around to the driveway, and their wedding guests—family and friends—followed.

Harlan stared at the gaudily decorated honeymoon car. It had had all the traditional, idiotic things done to it, including tin cans tied to the rear bumper. Beth grinned. "My brothers occasionally turn into adolescents."

"But that—that's not the Chevy."

"Oh, it's a Chevy, all right. It's just twenty-five *days* old, instead of twenty-five years."

She saw Harlan look at her, his expression a mix of love and anticipation of what the years ahead had in store for them. "But your car . . ."

"Retired." Beth smiled.

Eleanor Rockwood was the first to throw the rice. The chickens pounced, and Harlan and Beth, laughing, quickly escaped the ensuing melee.

TOO WILD TO WED? by Jayne Ann Krentz

Xavier Augustine had had his fiancée investigated to
find out if she were perfect wife material. Letty Conroy
had led a scandal-free life, but she determined that this
impudent man would find something wild and naughty
about her . . .

TERMINALLY SINGLE by Kate Jenkins

Family tradition dictated that Ashley Atwood would
be the next maiden aunt, and no man had ever tempted
her to fight her fate. Then sexy Michael Jordan crossed
her path and set about finding the fire which lurked
beneath her button-tight exterior.

A MAN FOR THE NIGHT by Maggie Baker

Lust – not love – turned Susan Harkness into the
passionate woman who had dragged Nick Taurage to
bed on their first – and only – date. She had wanted to
impress her colleagues and Nick was the most in-
triguing man she had ever met, but he was *not* the man
for her.

THAT STUBBORN YANKEE by Carla Neggers

Harlan Rockwood's ex-wife was a woman to be
approached with caution. Hot-tempered, dangerously
beautiful, Beth had already once ordered him out of
her life. He couldn't decide whether the thugs who
were out to get him or hiding out with Beth would be
the more hazardous to his health.

Spoil yourself next month
with these four novels from

— Temptation —

TANGLED LIVES by JoAnn Ross
(sequel to TANGLED HEARTS)

Reporter Mitch Cantrell wasn't about to let the sexy
and provocative singer, La Rubia, seduce General
Ramirez. Behind the green contact lenses and clinging
dresses, was a woman Mitch recognised. They had
once shared a dangerous assignment and nights of
passion – and he refused to let another man have her.

THE LAST GREAT AFFAIR by Kristine Rolofson

Arianna Simone couldn't believe her bad luck. First,
she went to the *wrong* wedding. Then, she was
kidnapped by the best man, who believed she was a
femme fatale out to ruin the nuptials!

BEN & LIZ & TONI & ROSS by Frances Davies

Tall, dark and handsome – I'd been waiting all my life
for a man like Ben Malloy. Only Toni, my roommate
and best friend, hadn't. She and I were like sisters –
always looking out for each other. Now that I'd found
my own hero, I had a choice to make: exclusive
friendship, or exclusive love.

LOVE COUNTS by Karen Percy

The cards told Lindsay that she was destined to meet
Mr. Right. But they neglected to mention that he
would be the wrong Mr. Right. Tim Reynolds – her
hunky business partner and a *younger* man.